THE CURSED CROW AND THE DEADLY HEX

POINT MUSE COZY PARANORMAL MYSTERY:
BOOK FOUR

KELLY ETHAN

 Created with Vellum

THE CURSED CROW AND THE
DEADLY HEX - BOOK FOUR

*There's a murder at Harrow House, a cruel crow
stalking old friends and a nosy librarian turned
sleuth.*
Let the mayhem begin...

With barely a breath to relax, Xandie Meyers and
her family of Harrow witches now must deal with a
new problem. *One that dropped dead at their feet.*

Someone is targeting old members of Elspeth
Harrow's, Morrigan Coven. The same Elspeth
Harrow who happens to be Xandie's long lost
Grandmother. People are dying and all signs point to
an inside job. Xandie has no choice but to swing into
Sherlock librarian mode.

Between bizarre accidents, a defanged vampire,
reanimated animal corpses and a search for a missing
doomsday device, Xandie barely has time to sniff out
the killer. A villain that's always two steps ahead.

*But whoever the murderer is they hadn't counted on
the stubbornness of Harrow witches and one nosy
librarian.*

ONE

"Death."

Alexandra Meyers, a.k.a. Xandie, librarian to the supernatural Great Library of Alexandria, winced as her banshee cousin screamed again.

"Death..." The wailing trailed off.

The crow plunged down, targeting Elspeth Harrow, a somewhat wicked hex-mad witch and matriarch of the Harrow family. Elspeth stepped back as the bird dropped, followed by a small murder of crows, all sinking to the ground around the Harrow witches in a bizarre, feathered minefield.

Elspeth stepped toward the first crow that had collapsed. The black-feathered body shimmered and formed into a naked, silver-haired old woman. Elspeth kneeled next to the woman's body and took her pulse, before turning and stomping inside. The front door to the house closed with a final and resounding bang.

"A dead crow shifter at your grandmother's feet after a banshee screams death isn't something you see every day." Lila Harrow gathered up a sobbing Holly, half banshee half witch, and bundled her inside Harrow House.

Xandie crouched next to the elderly woman. Jet black feathers lay tangled through her silver hair, and sweat had dried on the woman's emaciated body. The shifter looked like she'd flown long and hard, only to fall dead of exhaustion at Elspeth's feet. At the same time, her cousin saw their grandmother's death...

Elspeth exited the house, shovel in hand. She moved up and hovered close to Xandie. "Her name was Minerva Crow."

"You knew her?"

"We were part of the same coven, a long time ago." Elspeth stood, stony faced, then walked away to a pretty patch of Harrow garden where the sun filtered through the trees with soft rays and the rose petals smelled the strongest.

Xandie watched as Elspeth pushed the spade

deep into the rich soil. She was digging a grave for her departed friend.

Elspeth clicked her fingers, and the dead shifter hovered off the ground, then flew to her side. Lowering her down, Elspeth buried her.

Xandie joined her grandma, standing shoulder to shoulder with her. In a united sign of respect, they both remained silent for a few long moments.

"I need to make some phone calls. Update people." Elspeth dropped the spade and marched off.

"Are you going to tell us what's happening?" Xandie called out to her normally devious and full of life grandmother.

Elspeth stopped walking but didn't turn back to face Xandie. Her tone was so fierce and glacial, it was as if ice formed in the air between them. "When I'm ready, I'll let you know. Until then, tell those chattering witches to stay away from me." With that, Elspeth disappeared behind Harrow House.

And that was the Elspeth people equal parts hated and loved.

My grandmother.

TWO

"Last will and testament of Elspeth Harrow," Xandie read aloud and then cast an inquiring glance at her grandma. "Is there a reason I'm seeing this now instead of *after* you pass away?"

Snatching the document out of Xandie's hands, Elspeth rolled it up. "So, when I die a horrible death, you'll know three things." Elspeth moved a grinning Cheshire cat statue, turned it upside down, and wedged the will up inside the hollow cat.

"Three things?"

"That you're my favorite granddaughter, you'll inherit Harrow House, and..." Elspeth paused for effect. "And a devious, twisted villain murdered me."

Xandie sighed at her grandmother's antics. Something inside her had changed since the shifter had dropped dead at her feet and Xandie's cousin had very loudly proclaimed Elspeth's impending death. In fact, the last four weeks since the crow shifter had dropped dead at Elspeth's feet had been quiet. *Too quiet.* It was enough to silence any witch, Harrow or otherwise. But it was always best to have a healthy dose of fear when Elspeth, given to vocal interference in all her relatives' lives, turned into a creepy, non-talkative version of a brooding witch. "Who murders you?"

Elspeth waved a hand through the air. "Could be anyone. You wouldn't believe how many people I've upset in my long life."

"Oh yes, I would," Xandie muttered under her breath. It didn't pay to annoy the pre-eminent hexer in the region. "Let me recap. Because a shifter you once knew died at your feet, you think someone will murder you?"

"Because Minerva isn't the first of the coven to die in mysterious circumstances. She's the second." Elspeth patted the statue and turned expectantly to Xandie. "Well?"

"Ah, glad you aren't dead yet?" *Really, how does one answer that?*

"You're my sole beneficiary. You get lock, stock,

and witching candle." Elspeth settled her gaze on her granddaughter.

Xandie sat bolt upright and nodded vigorously. "Yep. Got it. Fantastic. But how about you tell me more about your coven and the person you think is trying to kill you? Because we both know you have a theory."

Elspeth sniffed and wandered the sitting room. "Nothing much to tell. We formed in World War Two. Did this and that and then I left to get married and have ungrateful babies."

"And you think someone is murdering members?" This was more information her grand-mother had volunteered in one sentence than she had in the last few months Xandie had known her. Elspeth loved mystique and mystery and preferred to haunt the shadows. Apparently, it was better to get the jump on your enemies and hex them. Before arriving in Point Muse, Xandie's life in college town Andrews with her dad had been calm...*and boring*. Harrows bought chaos and mayhem to her life, and Xandie was starting to see the attraction. She liked the drama. The dead bodies, she could do without.

"Let me guess, she changed the will again?" Lila poked her head into the sitting room.

"You, Lila Marie Harrow, are jealous you aren't

my favorite anymore." Elspeth glowered at her eldest granddaughter. The phone trilled from the kitchen. "That's mine." Elspeth scooted past Lila and made a break for the phone.

So much for being an old woman. She was spry enough for anyone half her age. Mind you, no one knew exactly how old Elspeth was. Any time someone asked her, she hexed them or lopped a year off the last age she'd told everyone. Her grandmother was short and slim, with close cropped, curly silver hair. Most of the time, a glaringly bright wig would sit atop her own hair, and Elspeth Harrow was never without her handy hip flask. Bedazzled, of course. Amber colored eyes completed the picture of a slightly devious and always dangerous elderly witch. Xandie might be a Meyers by name, but through her mother, Miranda Harrow, Elspeth's eldest daughter, she'd inherited her grandmother's lack of height and the Harrow eyes. All the Harrow women had the same amber eyes.

The three cousins shared a strong resemblance. Lila, the eldest, had curly, long brown hair. Xandie had shoulder length straight hair the same shade as Lila's. Holly, the youngest, also had the same shade hair in a smooth, short, chin-length bob.

As for Xandie's mother, she'd disappeared when

Xandie was five years old in a supposed tragic accident. Now, through a troll detective named Herman, hired by Xandie's deceased great-aunt Sera, the former librarian, Xandie had found out on top of all that, her mother wasn't dead or missing but had chosen to go underground and work for the suspicious human-only agency, ASP—the Anti Species Project. Her mother apparently had amnesia but had discovered ASP's rotten core and disappeared again. Only now, ASP was stalking Xandie and wanted to use her as bait to bring their rogue agent in. And if all that wasn't enough, she now had a dramatic Elspeth planning her will. *Good times.*

"Don't stress," Lila said. "She changes the will weekly. I thought we were due another rewrite with the dead crow and Holly wailing Elspeth's death sentence."

Poor Holly. It had horrified her after she realized she'd wailed at their grandmother. She was the quietest of the three cousins and hadn't bounced back from her vision like outgoing, over-dramatic Lila or bookish Xandie did after something dark and weird happened. Holly over-thought every move. Xandie, on the other hand, was stubborn and liked to jump in with both feet. "How's Holly coping?"

"Doing okay. Freaked, but glad her mom and

mine are on that singles' supernatural cruise they won. Everyone's relieved they aren't here to see the banshee fallout."

Out of the blue, the day after the crow episode, Aunt Amelia had received tickets in the mail for a cruise from a competition she couldn't remember entering. Elspeth convinced Amelia to take her sister and Colin, the talking pug, along with her. Winifred had been over the moon about the cruise, and Colin was excited to have the opportunity to peer up new skirts and pig out on all you can eat buffet food. Amelia took the chance for time away, and they all left soon after. "Elspeth told me they extended the cruise."

"Colin met a nice beagle. Aunt Winifred's preparing marriage vows as we speak." Lila frowned. "Has Elspeth mentioned anything else about the crow shifter yet?"

"Nope, just spoke about a coven they were all in years ago. Have you heard all the calls she's getting? She locks a silence hex around her every time she answers." Xandie stood and sidled toward the kitchen, Lila in tow.

Both girls paused around the corner, straining to hear Elspeth's phone call.

"Check on the others, and don't forget Henry,"

Elspeth whispered into the phone. "I don't care about anonymity. Warn the rest of them. Morrigan's being targeted. Get it done." Elspeth slammed the phone down, then noticed her granddaughters eavesdropping. "Eavesdroppers never hear good about themselves. And sometimes their ears fall off."

"And eavesdroppers also find out interesting tidbits about their secretive and devious grand-mother that she hasn't shared with her loving family who only want what's best." Lila folded her arms and glared.

"It's none of your business, baker girl." Elspeth sniffed and stomped past Lila and Xandie.

"Who's Morrigan?"

Elspeth had evidently forgotten to put a silence hex on the call, so they'd heard a few words. She'd mentioned a Henry, but it seemed that *Morrigan* had more emphasis. Xandie figured Elspeth might let something else slip that she could research with the Library. Especially if she badgered her.

"Morrigan is dead." The power in the house dimmed, and the shadows from every corner of the home gathered around Elspeth like a cloak.

"Cut the hag routine, Elspeth. We're all Harrows here." Lila snapped her fingers.

Shadows receded, but the power still fizzed off and on.

"Elspeth," Lila growled.

"Check your facts, sweetie. The power flicker isn't me." Elspeth grinned, teeth bared like a shark. "If the interrogation is over, I have underwear drawers to hex." The shadows swarmed Elspeth again as she faded out, disappearing with a high-pitched cackle.

"I hate it when she does the evil witch thing."

Xandie ignored her whining cousin and headed for the phone. If she could do a reverse phone call, it might tell her who Elspeth talked to, but the phone was dead again. Point Muse was renowned for spotty phone coverage because of the mess of ley lines running through the town. But somehow Elspeth could always call in and out whenever she liked.

"Forget it. I'm sure she's got some kind of mojo on it. We need to focus on what we heard. Henry and Morrigan and the fact someone's trying to kill them. Just like that crow shifter."

Lila was right, but something about the way Elspeth said Morrigan felt different, like a title, not a person. She nibbled a corner of her lip. "I'll ask Theo and the Library about Morrigan, see if they know anything." Her Library was sentient and contained all the knowledge of the supernatural world. As the current librarian, Xandie filled requests, copied information, shelved and coordinated appointments. If asked, the Library would help her with any information she needed as long as it was supernatural... and a crow shifter dropping dead qualified as supernatural.

"Your cat will lecture you about finding more corpses and then belch tuna breath everywhere."

Her cousin wasn't wrong. Xandie's lecturing furry feline had once been a binge-drinking Greek teenager until the Great Library of Alexandria had fought against a firebombing, demon-possessed Julius Caesar. Theophilus had ended up as Theo, a black cat guardian to the Library and every Librarian since. Especially everyone descended from Xandie's family. She was stuck with him. Unfortunately, no one else could hear his whining. The unlucky Librarian and the Library were the only ones to understand him. Although her Aunt Amelia, being an animal empath, could usually understand what he was feeling. "I have to swap that tuna out; it plays havoc with his indigestion."

Lila tapped her chin thoughtfully. "I think the Henry she's referring to might be Henry Strongarm.

He works at Point Muse Academy and is a full-time gym teacher. Maybe we should sleuth him out?"

At least Henry was nice and close and living in town. A thunderous knocking at the door derailed Xandie's thoughts.

Harrow House quivered and seemed to gather itself, waiting.

Lila reached the doorknob as Elspeth came flying down the stairs... *literally*.

A neon-pink, waist-length wig flew behind her as she rode a gust of wind down. "Dibs on the door. Why don't you girls go upstairs, quick smart?" Elspeth clicked her fingers.

Lila climbed the stairs, groaning and grabbing at the stair rail.

"Lila? Why are you groaning?"

"Because our damn grandmother hexed me. She's making me walk." With a moan, Lila disappeared upstairs.

Xandie ducked into the kitchen doorway and hid so Elspeth wouldn't see her. If her grandma hexed Lila to leave, then Elspeth didn't want them knowing who knocked. Thankfully, the Library protected her from all magic, so she could stay and spy.

With a twitch of her pink wig, Elspeth flung the

door open and scowled at the man in the doorway. "I can look after myself. Protect the others."

The man coughed. "That's what they told me. But since I have a pre-existing contact with a Harrow, they sent me."

Elspeth scoffed. "Please, none of my girls interact with the fuzz. Although..." Elspeth stopped to scan the man from coiffed top to shoe-shined toe. "The granddaughters might, or if you're into cougars, my youngest daughter would probably jump you."

"Alexandra Meyers and I met at her last place of work. The powers-that-be thought I might assist. Agent Ethan Jackson. *Paranormal Investigative Group.*" The agent nodded a greeting to Elspeth.

Xandie stared, shocked, at the agent. Why would he say they'd met at Andrews University? *My last job?* He wasn't one you'd forget. Except she had never seen him...or had she? Something familiar nagged at her. A sense of déjà vu. Had she run into him somewhere? She narrowed her gaze on the agent. He made a visual impact. Tall with dark brown hair that curled and puppy dog, brown eyes. Broad shoulders, a swimmer's waist, and muscles to tempt were all wrapped up in a package Elspeth would normally pinch on the bottom.

"Since you're a Forget-Me-Witch, obviously she

won't remember you. So, she doesn't count." Elspeth stuck her tongue out and moved to shut him out.

Agent Jackson slapped a hand on the door, but it didn't move anyway. Harrow House had a mind of its own and had decided they needed the agent. The door wasn't closing no matter what Elspeth did.

"Elspeth Harrow," the agent continued, "I'm sorry, but you're wanted for questioning in the deaths of Minerva Crowe and Hannah Lynch."

THREE

"Why do we always end up in jail?" Lila crouched and fiddled with Aggie Braun's toy wolf.

As soon as Elspeth had left the house, Lila had rushed downstairs, her grandma's compulsion spell dissolved, so they'd hightailed it down to the station.

Xandie grabbed the toy from Lila and stuck it on Aggie's desk. "Play nice. Aggie is a crony of Elspeth, and we don't want to annoy the police chief's mother before we spring Elspeth from the big house."

"Land sakes. Elspeth isn't under arrest." Aggie Braun, mother to Police Chief Zach Braun and in charge of Point Muse police station, glared around the room. "Toy boy agent was under pressure by his idiot bosses to bring Elspeth in. I heard the phone call. He tried to dissuade them, but apparently the

Paranormal Investigative Group bosses don't listen to smart junior agents."

"Not the way to encourage Elspeth's cooperation," Lila agreed.

Aggie waved the comments away. "My Zachy is sorting things out. The old girl will be home for 'Days of Our Witches' in no time."

"Days of Our Witches?" Xandie cocked an inquiring eyebrow at her cousin, Lila.

"Aggie and Elspeth's favorite soap opera on the Witchweb. They're addicted to it."

"What's going on? Is Elspeth in any danger? Should we get the aunts and Colin back from the singles' cruise?" Xandie gnawed on her nail.

"Elspeth Harrow is not under suspicion currently, but we need her to curtail her activities and stay close to home until we work things out."

That voice. That faint feeling of déjà vu... *again.* Xandie glared at the shaggy brown-haired man standing behind Elspeth. "Our grandmother is not a criminal. She's a fragile older lady and deserves respect."

"Have you met her?" The agent shook his head. "I'm sorry about how it happened, Xandie, but I didn't have a choice. My superiors wanted Ms. Harrow down at the station for questioning ASAP."

"How do you know my name, Mr. Agent?" Xandie took a step forward, hand on hips.

"My name is Ethan Jackson. And that's not important. What *is* important is that you came here and found what you were looking for."

What I was... Xandie glared at the annoying agent and let an idea wiggle its way out of her brain. "Go to Point Muse and stay out of the investigation," she mumbled, almost on audible autopilot. A blinding flash tore through her head. Xandie worked through the pain and wiggled out the memories she hadn't realized she had. "Damn you, Jackson," Xandie screeched. "You whammied me and made me move to Point Muse."

Jackson held up his hands. "Whoa, it was the best thing for you. Now you've got family and focus. You're the Librarian."

"You don't get to dictate and decide my actions like that." Xandie fumed at his high-handed behavior. It was all coming back to her in bits and pieces. The pixie drug dealer, the murders at her father's university in Andrews. And the oh so annoying Forget-Me-Witch and PIG agent, Ethan Jackson. "Hang on. The Library's supposed to make me immune to magic. How can a spell to forget work on me?"

"The Library didn't want you to know yet, I'm betting."

Elspeth hefted a lumpy tweed handbag onto her shoulder and accidentally connected with the side of Jackson's head. "She's always been a controlling harridan, that Library. Let's vamoose. The smell of prison food gives me reflux."

"Plus, she wants to binge watch the current season of her trashy soap opera," Lila offered in a fake whisper.

"Elspeth needs to lie low. No antics, no Witchshine and no hexing." Zach Braun closed the door to his office and strode toward Xandie and Lila. He paused in front of the agent and shot him a practiced sneer.

Zach Braun and Ethan Jackson were a study in contrasts. Zach had curly, sandy blond hair, thickly muscled shoulders, and piercing ice-blue eyes whereas Jackson had a lighter build and dark brown hair with brooding eyes. But both exuded alpha male, pain-in-the-behind tendencies.

"Chief Braun, we'll do our best. If you'll excuse me, the level of testosterone in this room is choking my delicate senses." Xandie did her own version of a sneer, grabbed Elspeth, and marched her outside to Lila's bakery van.

"Well, well. So that's Agent Jackson?" Elspeth smirked, back to her sarcastic self.

"What?" Xandie glared. "You knew about the spell he put me under?"

Elspeth climbed into the van and waited for Lila to start the engine. "I knew someone had whammied you from a few reports from friends. So, I had a general idea. But who knew a PIG could be so cute? Normally they're crusty old do-gooders."

Lila climbed in and turned the ancient engine over. The van coughed a few times before catching. "Feel the tension? Two males trying to exert dominance. I think Zachy boy's feeling the competition."

"There. Is. No. Competition. Now drive," Xandie commanded before sinking into her seat. The next few days would be epic headache material.

"Why are we at Lila's bakery instead of Harrow House, like the good law enforcement officer wants us to be?" Xandie sipped a milky hot tea. She'd swapped out Lila's addictive hot chocolate when the weight started creeping up on her hips. Heart's Delight Bakery was Lila's witchy superpower. Her gift went into her cooking, every morsel brimming with the positivity and self-love that powered her baking spells. Xandie wasn't a witch but a catalyst and the Librarian to the Great Library of Alexandria. Which, more often than not, meant her finding a dead body.

"That's why." Elspeth waved her fork. "Never do what people want you to. Don't be predictable, Xandie girl. It'll keep you alive longer." Elspeth shoveled a forkful of sinful chocolate cake into her mouth.

"And that's why Elspeth will outlive all of us. Won't you, old crow?" An older man with thinning reddish-gray hair stood beside Xandie's chair, massive arms crossed against his chest and a scowl on his face.

"Pure living sucks the life out of you, Buchanan."

Xandie looked from one frowning octogenarian to the other. "I take it you're friends?"

"No," both of them chorused.

"Buchanan is a do-gooder. They give me hives. Your grandfather was a friend of his."

"We worked together until he passed away and I retired."

Elspeth slammed her fork down on her plate. "Until he was killed, you mean. There was no passing, just messy death. And you're Paladin Inc. You're never retired."

Buchanan dropped his arms to his sides and fisted his hands. "I know you hate Paladin but get over it. Especially with what's going on right now. They can help you."

"I'm handling it," Elspeth spat the words out. "PIGS are involved. Everything will be fine. You stick to Henry. He's the one who needs your help. Not me. Go caretake something." Elspeth picked her plate up and stomped behind Lila's counter. She ignored the confused look Lila shot her grandmother's way.

"Monitor her. She's impulsive and never does what she's told. It's dangerous." Buchanan's pale blue eyes bored into Xandie.

"No offense, but if you know my grandmother, then you'd realize she's the most devious and dangerous person in this room."

He nodded. "Without a doubt, you're right, but she's too close to Morrigan to see clearly. Keep your wits about you, Librarian. You'll need it."

He spun to leave, but Xandie stopped him. "Wait. You mentioned Morrigan? Elspeth has told us nothing about her past. Who was Morrigan?" Xandie had a sudden brainwave. "Or what?"

"You're right. It's not a who, but a what. They were a coven of supernatural creatures. Different species, unique powers. The PIGs called them Morrigan's Crows, Morrigan for short. Elspeth was the coven leader, at least for a while. She was formidable and then it all ended...*badly*."

That sounded ominous. "How badly?"

"Body count badly. Elspeth left the coven and settled in Point Muse with your grandfather, Lucas."

"She won't talk about my grandfather unless it's insulting his do-gooder genes that we might have inherited from him."

Buchanan let out a sharp bark of laughter. "Sounds like Elspeth. She's always had a wild streak and the power to back it up. Surprisingly, they balanced each other out. She met him while doing an investigation for Paladin. But he was a straight-talking Paladin and Paladin Inc. was always a sore spot for her. Especially afterward." Buchanan nodded to Xandie and left as promptly as he had arrived.

"Why is our grandmother slamming pots and muttering curses in my kitchen?" Lila dropped into Elspeth's vacated chair.

"Because some guy called Buchanan spilled secrets." Xandie leaned forward and lowered her voice. "Morrigan is a coven, not a person, and apparently it comprised all kinds of supernatural species, not just witches. PIG called them crows or Morrigan for short. And our grandmother and deceased grandfather, Lucas, worked for an organization called Paladin Inc."

Lila whistled. "No wonder she's grumpy. Any mention of her husband or her past sends her into a tantrum."

"I have a few names to research. Morrigan and Paladin. She also mentioned that guy, Henry, again and something about caretaking?"

"That's because Buchanan is the live-in caretaker at the Academy." Holly leaned against Lila's chair and blew her short, choppy bangs out of her face. Her usual slick, dark brown bob was in finger-in-power-point disarray.

Xandie frowned. Her cousin was normally calm...*mostly*. When she wasn't squabbling with her chaos-causing, drama-queen cousin, Lila. However, today, she looked frazzled. "What's wrong? You look anxious."

Holly grimaced. "Some sicko kidnapped a heap of our pet clients. I've been all over town, knocking on the doors of our normal suspects. But no one knows anything."

"By pet clients, you mean pet bodies?" Holly worked at Elysian Fields Funeral Home. Being part banshee and having to prophesize death meant her cousin felt at home in the cemetery.

"Yes, my work buries pet bodies too." She sighed. "We had some in cold storage, spelled not to spoil. When we went to bury them this morning, the bodies had disappeared."

Lila wrinkled her nose. "Okay, that's sick. I can't believe you have people who steal bodies regularly."

Holly glowered at Lila. "Sometimes people donate their pets to us. We arranged for the Academy to have some for dissection and the alchemists in town like to grind things up for spells and rituals. We have permits for it."

"Still disgusting." Lila mimed a fake vomit with a finger in her open mouth.

Bristling, Holly jabbed her cousin in the shoulder. "You kill living things and cook them."

Lila rolled her eyes. "Baker. I bake. I don't kill anything."

"Whoa there, warring Harrows. We should probably focus on keeping Elspeth alive, instead of squabbling, right?" Xandie pointed at Holly. "Did you find out anything more about your vision of death?"

"Only that it's coming for her. Wants her bad. That's the only impression I get." Holly bit her lip.

"I'll keep trying, but my powers are spotty at best. I swear, as soon as I see anything, I'll tell you."

Xandie nodded. It was a long shot as Holly was only just coming into her powers. Delayed maturity, Elspeth called it. Speaking of Elspeth... "Lila and I have to head to the Academy and speak to this Henry from the coven. You grab Elspeth and go home. Wait with her until we get back. And for goodness sakes, don't let her out."

Holly pulled a face but agreed and stomped into the kitchen to pry Elspeth away from pot banging.

Lila nodded for her waitress to take over and stood. "Let's get this done. Who knows how long it will be before Elspeth reduces her to a babbling mess?"

Xandie followed behind Lila as they ducked outside to her cousin's decrepit bakery van. Elspeth and Holly rubbed each other the wrong way. Mind you, Elspeth rubbed everybody the wrong way.

Somehow, they had to keep Elspeth on home detention, safe and sound.

Not to mention keep our sanity intact...

FOUR

"The smell of gym socks is strong in this one." Lila coughed and waved a hand in front of her nose as they walked through the locker room.

"Kids stink. It's a fact of life." Xandie pointed to a darkened hallway off the locker room. "His offices are there somewhere."

"Why is it so dark? School's only been out for an hour and it's already deserted." Lila shivered and shoved Xandie ahead of her. "As Librarian, you should go first. Celebrate with pride your career achievements, cousin."

Xandie snickered at Lila's silliness. Truth be told, considering her track record with bodies, her cousin had a valid reason for hanging back. "Fine, but you call the police if we find a corpse."

A voice sounded from the shadows. "No corpses here. Can I ask what you're doing on Academy premises?"

Xandie and Lila swung around in shock, and Xandie was surprised at her own reaction. Her hands had curled into fists, ready to fight instead of her previously natural instinct to flee.

"Sorry to scare you, ladies. I'm Henry Strongarm, the gym teacher here. What can I do for you?"

Bingo. Just the man they were stalking. Xandie stepped out from behind Lila and scrutinized Henry. Thick gray beard, heavily muscled shoulders, with no hint of old age sag. A strong, large nose dominated his face, and he had a bald head with dark brown eyes. Xandie held her hand out. "Hi, I'm Xandie Meyers, the Librarian. Elspeth Harrow is my grandmother. This is my cousin, Lila Harrow. We'd like to ask you a few questions."

A large grin split Henry's face. "Why didn't you say that first? Elspeth was a good friend of mine once."

"Seriously? Can't imagine Elspeth taking the time to be nice to anyone, let alone make a friend," Lila said, choking back a laugh.

He nodded. "She's a live-wire. Why don't we get settled in my office? That way, the spell chuckers won't disturb us." Henry strode down the hallway and opened the door at the far end of the corridor.

"Spell chuckers?" Xandie whispered to Lila.

Henry directed the girls to two chairs. "Powered kids throwing spells at each other. It's a big competition here. Finals are in a week."

"Isn't that dangerous?" Xandie had seen Elspeth chuck a spell or two, and it was never pretty.

"We put binders on them. No maiming or killing. How can I help Elspeth's granddaughters?"

Xandie exchanged a look with Lila, both of them unsure what to actually ask.

"Is it about Minerva dying?" he prodded Xandie, giving her an opening.

She nodded. "We're worried about Elspeth."

"Seeing Minerva die would have rocked poor Elspeth. Grief must eat at her. She was always such a sensitive witch." Henry sniffed and rifled through his desk drawers until he found a tissue.

Wracked with grief wasn't a term she'd have used in connection with her mayhem-loving grandmother. Sensitive witch wasn't either.

"Oh, yes." Lila bent forward, an earnest expression on her face. "We want to help her. Make sure she's safe. But we need all the details."

Nodding, he made a dramatic production of

getting up and closing his office door. "You can't be too careful. Ears everywhere." He settled back into his chair. "I'm only cleared to give you a little information. Paladin and the Paranormal Investigative Group are tightfisted when it comes to control over case details and information."

Why were the feds and Paladin involved? What exactly was Paladin Inc.? Xandie hadn't realized she'd spoken aloud until Henry answered.

"Paladin Inc. was formed centuries ago. Originally made up of Templars, they served a higher cause and multiple gods. They dealt with Armageddon events. Anything magic-oriented that threatens the end of the world. Templars and the PIGs look after the small stuff."

"What's that got to do with Elspeth?" Armageddon certainly sounded like her grandmother, though. Xandie mulled the idea over. Buchanan, the old guy at Lila's café, mentioned she worked for Paladin briefly while their grandfather had been a Paladin agent. And Elspeth named Buchanan a Paladin too. "We just found out our grandfather worked for Paladin Inc."

Henry clapped his massive hands together. "Yes, they worked together. That's how they met. They were both investigating Morrigan and our boss,

Albert Proctor. Of course, that backfired, and the coven fractured."

"Why?" Lila asked.

"Nothing I can go into. Let's say Morrigan had a specific function during the war. Some people didn't appreciate our efforts and our processes, especially when it came to how Elspeth handled things. Maybe someone decided to do something about it. Your grandmother upset people with her investigation and Morrigan had enemies. In fact, Elspeth upset the coven too." He cracked his knuckles and stood. "The chuckers have probably arrived, so I should get out there and supervise."

Xandie followed her cousin but stopped to ask one more question. "You said no one appreciated the coven's efforts, especially Elspeth's. Was there anyone inside the coven who particularly hated her?"

Henry dropped his jovial smile and assessed Xandie. "Smart girl." He snapped his fingers. "That's right, you're the Librarian, aren't you?"

Xandie nodded and waited for him to continue.

"Elspeth has always been blunt and devious, and after the coven broke, some of its members were angry with her for a particularly long time. Especially Lucien and Hell. I don't think they ever believed or forgave her betrayal. Although Lucien eventually made up with Elspeth. I think hating her betrayal became too much, and he extended a truce and is in contact with her still. Then again, I wondered if he'd always known what she and Lucas were doing and acted betrayed when the sordid business came to light. The vampire drama-queen was always good at acting. Minerva always sided with Elspeth and never held a grudge, but other members hated her. Once upon a time, we were all thick as thieves. I really have to check on the chuckers." Henry shuffled them into a hallway filled with the discordant yells of warring teenagers.

"Lucien and Hell who?" Xandie pressed the oversized gym teacher for details.

"Lucien Benoit and Hellacious Whitburn. Oh, and Bridget hated Elspeth for a very long time too. They always clashed even before the coven break-up. If you'll excuse me?" Henry gestured to a teenager stuck to a wall with green gooey material and then took off to help.

Xandie avoided glowing concoctions held by bloodthirsty teenage hellions. "We have a few more names. I can hit the Library and see what it has on them."

Lila agreed. "You'll probably get more from the Library than you will from Elspeth."

"What do you mean, access restricted?" Xandie glowered at her Library. The supernatural contents of the Great Library of Alexandria had moved itself to Point Muse. Her family had been Librarians to the Great Library since the beginning. The font of all supernatural knowledge... *Normally*.

"I'm the Librarian. I should be able to access all information."

"Unless the Library decides you shouldn't have it." Theo snickered and batted his pet imp, Horatio, like a bouncy ball.

Growling at her feline guardian's antics, Xandie prowled the room. Since moving here and solving her Great-Aunt Sera's murder, the Library and Theo, her prickly, snarky black cat, had quickly wound their way into her heart and life. Meeting the PIG agent, and realizing he'd made her forget her introduction to the supernatural world, explained why she'd accepted the weird of Point Muse so readily.

Xandie trailed a hand over a shelf and touched

the spine of a leather-bound book. The Library, filled to the brim with shelves, books, and scrolls, had a warm, welcoming feeling. Thick rugs covered polished wood floorboards. Heavy timber reading tables and large comfy chairs dotted the room. A small office and stationery room sat wedged in a quiet corner and the Library appointments book that held her denied written information request sat open on a scarred wooden antique desk.

Every day, Xandie would collect requests for information or access and write them in the appointment book. The Library decided when or who would have access to its inner knowledge. Little notes from the Library would appear in the book for Xandie. Just like the one denying her access.

"Why would the Library bar my access to coven records?" Xandie poked Theo in his rib cage and smiled as he yowled and leapt onto a chair.

"Cut it out, human. I'm ticklish."

"Answer me, furball."

Theo arranged himself on the green velvet chair. "Fine. The Library, in conjunction with Paladin Inc., blocked all access to coven information. It has a rating of *Armageddon eyes only.*"

Xandie threw herself into a chair opposite the big desk. "And..."

"You can only open it if Armageddon is pending."

Foiled. But what if she researched the two coven names Henry had mentioned? "Library, do you have any knowledge of Benoit and Whitburn?"

The crystal pendant lights above Xandie flickered wildly as two books flew into her lap. Xandie patted the arm of the chair. "Thanks, Library. I guess I just had to rethink the question." Xandie picked the topmost book, which happened to be the largest, and opened it to the *Contents* page. "A ranking of vampire houses and clans." Xandie frowned. Obviously this meant at least one of the two names she'd mentioned was a vampire.

She ran a finger down the chapter headings. The name Benoit or Whitburn failed to appear. Taking a punt, she held the book open in her hands. "Can you give me a helping hand, Library?" The pages fluttered and then flipped open near the back of the book. Xandie grinned her thanks. "Says here one of the few notable vampire houses that served with distinction during various armed conflicts is the Benoit clan."

Henry had mentioned that Morrigan was formed during World War Two. Xandie continued, "And it must be noted, House Benoit helped bring about the end of Hitler and his obsession with the supernatural. House Benoit was the only vampiric house that volunteered a high-ranking member to a secret project under the Paranormal Investigative Group. The project gathered a variety of supernatural entities to police and actively bar Hitler from access to the supernatural." *This has to be them.* The Morrigan Coven Elspeth had been part of.

"Lucien Benoit, of indeterminate age, but outstanding morals and bravery, fought honorably in service to the greater good. The subsequent investigation into ethical questions of their practices and the later death of Albert Proctor, head of the division, has tarnished his contribution. The disappearance of the Morpheus Amulet and the desertion of the coven head, Elspeth Harrow, ruined the coven, and all members disbanded after she resigned." She'd quit? What happened to her leaving to settle and raise a family?

"That old witch never mentioned the coven or why she left?" Theo stretched his paw out and let Horatio clamber onto his back.

"Nope. Lips sealed tight. But something happened, and I think it's about that amulet." Xandie scanned the passage, but it mentioned nothing else. She swapped to the other book.

"Necromancers and other denizens of Dark Magic." *Upbeat title.* Xandie snickered and randomly opened to a page, hoping the Library's goodwill would stretch to more information on the coven members. "Necromancers have long been drawn to the shadowed side of magic. They are partial to meddling in the human world and encouraging dark practices by mortals. This is most evident during contentious times of human history. Necromancers do not enjoy notoriety, though, and stay in the shadows and manipulate. Except for a few names like Hellacious Whitburn, they are largely anonymous." So, necromancers were puppeteers, pulling strings and staying in the background, hidden. What made Whitburn so different?

"Whitburn started in the employ of Adolf Hitler but grew concerned with Hitler's obsession with the supernatural and particularly with a certain dark artifact. The coven leader approached him, and he became a double agent. Whitburn would contact the special projects group at PIG and telegraph Hitler's movements and the artifacts he had stolen. He soon became a full-time member of the Morrigan Coven and reported directly to them. The coven foiled Hitler's attempts to use an Armageddon level dark artifact, and soon after, Hitler fell. The artifact and Whitburn reportedly disappeared shortly after."

"All of your grandmother's close friends are suspiciously dodgy." Theo yawned and rolled, almost squishing a slumbering Horatio.

"Are you surprised?" Xandie went back to reading out loud. "Whitburn then surfaced in the nineties in Silicon Valley, where he headed up a necromantic-based video game company. He cashed in on the humans' lust for computer graphics and blood and became the owner of a well-known gaming company, Necro Inc. He is currently the only documented billionaire necromancer."

"Like I said. Dodgy. Never trust anyone who plays with the deceased."

Xandie closed the books and piled them onto the table. "What about Holly? She works with the dead daily."

"Like I said." Theo sneered at Xandie before a loud sneeze erupted from him, followed by another. "Speaking of the dead, I smell embalming fluid."

Holly stood in the Library's doorway. "We have a problem."

It was never good when a prophesying banshee and Harrow witch told you they had a problem.

That's normally code for a body.

FIVE

It *was* a body. Just not a Harrow one. Xandie kneeled next to Holly in the same locker room she'd been in earlier. "Want to tell me how you got a look-in with the body? Chief Braun would have a conniption if he knew we were here."

Holly gestured to the bear shifter deputies behind her, Caleb and Melody Braun. Brother and sister to Chief Zach Braun. "He already knows but wants us to have a look before the PIGs get here."

"Which could be any minute." Xandie peered at the gym teacher, Henry, friend to Elspeth and ex-Morrigan Coven member. "Poor guy. Lila and I talked to him only a few hours ago. Do we know what killed him yet?"

Using a gloved hand, Holly lifted Henry's arm

and rotated it carefully before placing it down. "Elspeth would know better. But considering he was about thirty pounds heavier when I saw him at Lila's bakery a few days ago, I'd say an energy transference or leaching hex."

Holly was right. The poor man looked like his skin was one size too large for him. "Awfully coincidental, don't you think? A few hours after Lila and I spoke to him, he's dead?"

"Awfully. But then you might not have been the only Harrow visiting him." Agent Ethan Jackson held up Elspeth's bedazzled hipflask. "The police found this under his body."

Xandie straightened and glared at the agent. "You have no proof that's my grandmother's. It could belong to anyone."

Jackson turned the flask around and showed Xandie the pink rhinestone-embossed name of Elspeth.

"Could be any Elspeth who likes to bedazzle her hipflask." Holly stood in stubborn Harrow solidarity with Xandie.

"It's pretty damning. I need to question Elspeth Harrow again." Two other black-suited agents stepped up next to Agent Jackson.

"This is none of your business." Xandie scowled at the intrusive agent.

"I'm sorry, but the Paranormal Investigative Group has jurisdiction here."

"Actually, sonny, Henry was in Paladin Inc. custody. So, it's Paladin

business now, and we're choosing to involve local law enforcement." Buchanan, Paladin agent and Elspeth's nemesis, stood in the hallway close to Henry's office, a wide grin on his face.

"Well, now. I'm thinking we need to send that flask out for prints. Don't you, Zachy bear?" Agatha Braun stood in the doorway, her large bear arms crossed in front of her.

Zach Braun, Point Muse Police Chief, stood next to her, scowling. "I think you're all contaminating my crime scene and need to get out. Starting with the agents from PIG."

"If that's the way you want to play it. But we could help each other." Agent Jackson dropped the flask into Chief Braun's gloved hand before stomping off with his agent back-up following.

Chief Braun handed the evidence off to his mother, who bagged it, and then he nodded to his deputy siblings. "Next time, no PIGs unless we okay it." Braun didn't wait for an agreement before walking over to Holly. "What do you think?"

"Autopsy might tell you more, but I'm sure the murder weapon was an energy leach hex. Sucks the energy out of him and siphons off to the hex user. Henry would have died of heart failure as his organs shut down."

Buchanan dropped the smile and walked over to Henry. "This is my fault. I was his handler. I should have paid more attention to his whining and complaints."

Henry hadn't struck Xandie as a whiner. In fact, he seemed easygoing. Not the type to complain. "What do you mean?"

"The last few days. He kept saying he felt like someone was watching him. He complained that everything was out of place in his office. I just put it down to student pranks." Buchanan opened his eyes wide, as if something had only just occurred to him, then he bolted to Henry's office.

After Xandie exchanged a glance with Holly, she followed the Paladin. Buchanan headed straight for an old statue of Hercules that lay on its back on Henry's desk.

He grabbed the statue and turned it upside down. "Dammit. Whoever killed him knew Henry had a portion of the amulet." He glared at the empty space inside the statue before slamming it back on the desk.

"You're talking about the Morpheus Amulet. The dark artifact that Hellacious Whitburn double-crossed Hitler for?"

Buchanan shook his head. "Nope. At no stage do I confirm or deny that Henry had a portion of the amulet or that your grandmother does too. No confirmation here." He scowled at the cousins. "Got it?"

Holly nodded vigorously and elbowed Xandie until she followed suit.

"I need to get hold of Paladin Inc. Tell that stubborn grandmother of yours I'll be around later. Now get." Buchanan pointed at the door.

"We're getting." Xandie dragged Holly out into the hallway, shutting the late Henry's office door behind her.

Holly blinked owlishly at Xandie. "Why did we vacate so quickly? Buchanan obviously has more information that we could pry out of him."

"Pick your moments, cousin." Xandie slapped Holly on the back. "Plus, he'll have more information when he tangles with Elspeth. Then we can pry."

"No prying into Paladin Inc. They frown on that." Aggie Braun stood at the top of the hallway.

"Of course, wheedling, whining, and the fluttering of eyelashes is all aboveboard."

If only Zach Braun would be as easygoing as his mother. Xandie slipped up to Aggie and gave her a quick hug. "Thanks for making Chief Cranky-Pants work with us."

"Oh, you." Aggie laughed and gave Xandie a quick squeeze before letting go. "Zachy has a lot on his plate, and Elspeth's safety is the most important. *You* can work unofficial angles that he can't. He saw the benefits of a Harrow witch meddling pretty quickly." Aggie motioned for the women to follow her as a swarm of leather-clad men filled the locker room.

Holly channeled her cousin Lila's confidence and drama queen attitude and pinched her cheeks before smiling widely at a hottie. The blond man nearest Holly shot her smirk and a wink, then continued his examination of Henry's body.

Aggie grabbed Holly and Xandie's elbows and moved them away from the locker room. "Stay away from the leather brigade. Those are tier one Paladin field agents. They won't hesitate to pull the trigger, then spread peace and love over your remains."

Xandie peeked back into the locker room. So,

that was the organization her grandfather had worked for?

"Geez, no wonder Elspeth married one. They're hotties."

Aggie tapped Holly's nose. "Down, bloodhound. Paladins only concern themselves with apocalyptic events. Most of them are the love them and leave them type."

"And our grandfather?" Xandie pressed Aggie for information. Her grandfather was a shrouded mystery Elspeth barely spoke of, except to rail at the goody-two-shoes genes her kids and grandkids had inherited from him.

Students of all shapes and sizes and supernatural races stepped around the older bear shifter. "Lucas Munro was just like those men in there, at least until he met Elspeth. He had the classic Paladin do-no-wrong streak, but Elspeth's wild, chaotic life centered him somehow. Same for her, but just the opposite, I suppose. Damn shame when he died. I think it broke something in your grandmother."

"How did she meet him?" Holly had forgotten the smorgasbord of unattainable hunks in the locker room in exchange for juicy Elspeth gossip.

"Something to do with an issue in her old coven. Lucas had to work with her, and it snowballed from there. Eventually, they settled in Point Muse and had your mothers."

"What turned Elspeth into a cranky hexer?" Xandie couldn't imagine the Elspeth she knew now settling down and having kids all those years ago. But evidence stated otherwise.

"Paladin declared Lucas inactive. But something big was brewing, and they called in all the most powerful agents for a pow-wow." Aggie paused and shook her head sadly. "Some kid related to Elspeth's old boss snuck into Paladin Headquarters with an absorber hex. Once it sucked in enough electrical energy, he exploded himself. There were no survivors."

Holly gasped, hand to mouth. Tears pooled in her eyes. "That's horrible. No wonder she's such a witch."

"Your mothers were young when it happened, so Elspeth raised the kids by herself. But she was never the same. Neither was Paladin Inc. They spent years building up their numbers again."

"So, how did Buchanan miss the explosion at Headquarters?" Xandie wondered out loud.

Buchanan stood in the locker doorway, glowering at Aggie and the Harrows. "Because I was in the hospital with bullet wounds from an attack the day before. Not that it's any of your business. How about you focus on Elspeth's safety instead?"

Aggie straightened with a cough. "Head back to Harrow House. I'll let you know if we find anything. Zachy's sending Melody for protection."

"Braun doesn't need to send a deputy out. I have agents on the way out there."

Aggie directed a glare at Buchanan. "Melody is a shifter, a deputy, and Zach's sister. She can help. Call your leather lads off." Aggie wiggled her fingers at Holly and Xandie to get them moving.

Buchanan grunted and watched as Xandie dragged Holly away.

Xandie rubbed the back of her neck. The last few weeks, she'd had constant goosebumps and chills along her spine. The ominous foreboding that something or someone was just around the corner, waiting for her...or stalking her. Those horrid ASP agents hung around Point Muse like a nasty stench. They wanted to use her as bait for her errant run-away mother. For that matter, could the prickling of her neck mean her mother had regained some of her memories and was watching? Or was this all connected to Elspeth? Giving up on her theories of stalkers, Xandie turned to the issue in front of her.

Harrow House stood like a majestic purple and blue Victorian grand dame. Harrow ancestors had built the house a long time ago, and once upon a time, it had overflowed with Harrow witches. Now it housed a cranky octogenarian witch, her candle-obsessed middle daughter, and her banshee witch granddaughter, Holly. And one annoyed deputy bear shifter, camped out on the porch.

"She won't let me in. Apparently, I'll shed on her clean floors." Melody Braun, deputy and sister to bear shifter Police Chief Zach Braun, sat on a porch step, tapping her colorful painted nails on the wood.

"Do bear shifters shed?" A question Xandie never thought she'd have to ask.

"Only my summer coat and that's just old fur. It doesn't count."

"I've seen a brown bear shed and it ain't pretty. I just cleaned this floor. No bear shedders allowed," Elspeth yelled through the closed door.

Melody rolled her eyes and pulled out a nail file. "It's fine. I'll sit here. Just make sure she doesn't do a runner out the back door."

"She's old. Over eighty or ninety as far as we can work out since she lies about her age. How far could she get?" Seriously, extended lifespans were pretty cool. Elspeth rocked at least ninety but looked and acted like she was in her sixties. A spry one at that.

Holly stared, shocked, at Xandie. "How long have you known Elspeth for?"

"Excellent point." Xandie stepped up to the porch and banged on the front door.

"I don't need what you're selling. Move along, or you can spend the rest of your life with zombie fleas," Elspeth shouted through the door.

"First thing—zombie fleas, really? Second, Henry's dead," Xandie yelled back at her cantankerous grandmother. Sometimes blunt force trauma was the only way to get through to the old crone.

There was dead silence until Harrow House's door creaked open. Elspeth stood blinking in the doorway. Turning, she kicked the door frame. "Stupid house with a mind of its own. I tell you who to let in." Elspeth stomped off to the kitchen, Xandie and Holly behind her.

"Well, look what the cat dragged in." Lila sprawled at the massive scarred wooden dining table, munching on a slice of cold pizza.

Holly stomped over to the table and snatched Lila's slice of pizza. "We're working hard examining corpses and you're gorging on pizza?"

"Hey." Lila nabbed her slice back. "This is danger pay for dealing with Elspeth."

"It's about to get worse." Xandie patted Lila on the head and zeroed in on a lurking Elspeth.

"I can't believe the house let you witchy slackers in. I think it's time Harrow House and I had a serious conversation." Elspeth bared her teeth and tapped rainbow-colored fake talons on the kitchen counter.

Xandie grabbed Elspeth and shuffled her off to a small, quiet sitting room.

"Henry died of an energy leach hex, and his part of the Morpheus Amulet is missing. Buchanan is circling the Paladin agent wagon, and everyone is fighting over jurisdictional issues with the Para-normal Investigative Group. Prevailing theory is you're either a future victim or the perp. It's time to come clean, Elspeth." Xandie purposefully stood in the doorway, blocking Elspeth's escape. A gust of wind rattled the windows in the sitting room, and Xandie flinched, ruining her tough Librarian inter-rogator image.

Elspeth snorted at Xandie's antics and settled back into a padded rocking chair in front of a large picture window. "I'm sorry to hear about Henry. He was a relatively competent gym teacher. I'm sure Point Muse Academy will miss him."

"And you? He was a friend and, according to Henry, a colleague, once upon a time."

Elspeth stared out the window. "A long time ago, in another life." She sniffed and turned back to Xandie. "Not that it's any of your beeswax, nosy."

Xandie gritted her teeth. Elspeth was not a caring, sharing grandmother type. But even Xandie recognized defensive delay tactics when they slapped her in the face. Xandie rapped a knuckle on the door frame. "Help me out here, house."

Harrow House shuddered, and a smooth wall appeared where a moment before there had been a doorway.

Xandie smiled victoriously. "Spill it, wicked Harrow. Because you aren't getting out of here until you do."

Elspeth gave a push with her feet and set her chair rocking. "Everyone's a drama queen. I don't know where you get it from. Yes, Henry was a coven member and a friend. Same with Minnie. Minerva Crow."

"The shifter who died here?"

"Yeah, the crow. She always believed the best in me." Elspeth snorted. "More fool her."

"How many members of the coven are dead?"

"Henry and Minerva died here in Point Muse.

Buchanan told me Hannah Lynch died in a car bomb a few months ago. And Hellacious is missing."

"Hannah Lynch?"

"She was an assistant to that criminal, Albert Proctor, my old boss." Too restless to sit in her rocking chair, Elspeth hoisted herself up and paced in front of the picture window, peering and tapping on the glass every so often.

Xandie joined her grandmother. Light disappeared quickly as night took hold. The wind had picked up, and the occasional gust of rain beat against the house. Elspeth seemed riveted by the darkening landscape outside. Anything to escape giving up her secrets. "How many coven members are left?"

"There were six of us in total. Two of us are dead, one missing, so that means three of us are left."

"And Hannah?"

"She was only support staff to the coven, and Albert Proctor is dead—suicide at the end of World War Two." Elspeth frowned and moved closer to the window, tracking something scurrying around outside. Electricity flickered off and on. A blink of darkness followed by blazing lights again. Harrow House shivered an apology.

"Why is someone killing for the pieces of the Morpheus Amulet?"

Elspeth answered on autopilot, her concentration consumed by whatever was outside. "Hell obsessed over it. Hitler, too, and in the end, Proctor. We broke the amulet into parts because it's less effective in pieces. Each separate chunk can send a person into a deep sleep. It increases the dream state until dreams turn into nightmares. Eventually, the nightmares overload the nerve centers, and the subject literally dies of fear. Formed into one part, the amulet can flashbang entire countries. That's why Hitler wanted it. Who knows what Proctor had planned?"

"And that's why your coven formed to stop it?"

"We tried. But sometimes the end doesn't justify the means."

"Something went wrong in the coven? Did it have anything to do with your boss?"

Elspeth finally turned away from the windows and stared straight at Xandie. "He was stealing artifacts, dealing on the black witch market. He wanted the amulet, but no one believed me except Paladin."

"And Grandfather?"

"He was my handler. I was undercover, trying to expose Proctor. The coven dug deeper and deeper into dark magic to stop Hitler. Eventually, Proctor and Hitler killed themselves, and Whitburn disappeared."

"Did you or Whitburn take the amulet?"

Elspeth snorted. "No. That was just a rumor. Your grandfather broke the artifact into pieces. Henry, Bridget Doyle, Lucien Benoit, and I each had a piece. And then we dispersed."

"And now someone is killing you off one by one for your amulet pieces."

"Aren't you gonna ask me if I killed my friends?" Elspeth grabbed for her hipflask and then grimaced.

"Hipflask missing?"

"Must've put the damn thing down somewhere, or the house hid it."

"Try looking under Henry's dead body. At least that's where the PIGs found it."

Elspeth rolled her eyes. "You can't think I'd murder Henry? Not to mention, would I really leave evidence behind if I did?"

"You certainly wouldn't leave your name-bedazzled hipflask at the crime scene. And if you wanted someone dead, they would be. There'd be no staged crime scene. So, no, I don't think you killed your friends."

Elspeth's cackle coincided with a flash of lightning that lit up the yard and the mushy face of someone's obviously dead cat.

A dead cat that was staring straight at Xandie through the glass. Xandie let out a piercing scream and leapt back, dragging Elspeth with her.

Pounding on the wall-covered doorway echoed through the compact sitting room. Harrow House shuddered, the doorway appeared again, and Holly and Lila collapsed on the ground at their grandmother's feet.

Powers surged and lights in the room blew with a metallic pop, a rain of glass from the light bulb showering everyone.

"This isn't going to end well." Elspeth's words dropped into the room like an anchor, tethering the Harrows together in the darkness.

Xandie couldn't help but agree that a dead cat and a power-stripped Harrow House was a recipe for let's-kill-Elspeth-Harrow.

SIX

"They're all around us. The house is surrounded," Lila whispered to Xandie and then ducked back down to the floor, hiding beneath the windowsill.

Xandie raised her head and peeked over the sill. A half-eaten moose and a chipmunk missing its furry tail had joined the dead cat. All the animals had glowing green eyes. She fought a heave as the lightning faded away, leaving the zombie animals covered by night again.

"Do you have any idea what's going on, Elspeth?" Xandie waited for an answer but instead, frantic mouth-breathing from her terrified cousins met her question. "Elspeth? Please tell me you haven't deserted us and left us for zombie snacks?"

"She never did like you, Lila," Holly whispered to her cousin.

"Seriously? You're turning on me already? We've barely been in the dark for ten minutes. Besides, aren't *you* Death Girl? Can't you do anything about the zombie critters?" Lila jabbed a finger at the window, only to yank it back when something scraped the glass next to her hand.

"I'm a banshee. I have visions of death. I don't Pied Piper dead animals."

"This is proof that Harrows don't play well together." Xandie gritted her teeth for a moment, then took a deep breath and continued, "We need to find Elspeth and protect her since she's the target."

"I think I'd be safer by myself, truthfully." Elspeth stood in the doorway, holding one of the numerous candles that Winifred had made and slotted into every bare space in the house that she could find. In her other hand, she carried a short sword which she twisted so it shone in the candlelight.

"Should our evil hexing grandmother be holding a sharp implement of death?" Lila nudged Xandie. "You take it off her."

Xandie reared back and shook her head. "Why

should I take it off her? Holly's her favorite—she can take it."

"Hell no. It's not my time to go yet. I'm too young. She only likes me because I keep her Bedazzler up and running. Plus, I bribe her with alcohol and chocolate, so it's fake love. Xandie's the Librarian —she can do it."

Elspeth tapped her foot on the wood floor. "Maybe you all should get away from windows that could shatter at any second?"

With a squeal, all three women scrambled to their feet and hid behind Elspeth.

"Space, girls. Space." Elspeth elbowed her way to fresh air. She narrowed her gaze and waved her sword in the air. "Warrior up, offspring. Grab something pointy before the decomposing overrun us."

Lila rolled her eyes. "Why do I feel like you're enjoying this debacle?"

Holly grabbed a couple of her mother's candles and lit them off Elspeth's burning one.

"Harrows are all about action and after hermitting for the last week, she's probably bored. And you know what happens when Elspeth's bored." Holly handed the lit candles out and disappeared into the kitchen.

Lila shuddered. "A bored Harrow equals chaos and mayhem and sometimes, a body or two."

"Nothing wrong with a healthy dose of mayhem." Elspeth pointed at the chipmunk chittering at the window. "Of course, that kind of mayhem is disease-ridden. Not my style at all."

"Here." Holly reappeared and shoved two sharp carving knives, handles first, at her cousins.

Xandie took the zombie-slicing knife gingerly and juggled the candle as she tried to find a comfortable position for both.

"Would be kind of great if I didn't need to use the candle and knife at the same time. Any spell that will give us some light instead?"

Elspeth beamed at Xandie. "You *are* my favorite granddaughter. I have just the thing." She snapped her fingers and mumbled a few words under her breath. A glowing halo outlined her head. Then, one by one, a new circle of light appeared over the cousins as Elspeth pointed a finger at each of them. A nimbus of multicolored light formed over Lila and Holly's heads. A gold ball of light formed over Xandie's.

Elspeth cackled and pointed at Xandie. "All you need are wings, girly. Wait until Paladin Inc. gets a look at you three."

"Stuff that cackle back down your throat and get ready." Lila snuffed the candles out, then dumped them on a chair.

Xandie did the same. Elspeth did nothing without a devious reason. This was probably a malicious jab at Paladin Inc. "What's next? You've obviously got a plan, Elspeth. So, what do we do now?"

A guttural roar from the front porch answered Xandie. She clapped a non-knife wielding hand over her mouth and bolted for the front door, with the others following close behind. She yelled over a shoulder, "We forgot Melody. We left her on the front porch."

Xandie reached the door and found a furry bear spread-eagled on the porch, covered in reanimated dead animals. A squirrel with holes in its fur chittered trash talk at the newcomers.

"Nothing worse than an unwelcome guest who won't take a hint. Not to mention shedding body parts." Elspeth lifted her short sword and swung. The squirrel's head flew through the air and landed next to Melody.

Melody-bear moaned and turned to Xandie, showing the whites of her eyes.

"What are you waiting for? An invitation to slice

and dice the unholy furry dead?" Elspeth waded in with the sword, swinging left and right.

Xandie shrugged, then surged forward. She thrust with her knife and skewered a dead one-eyed crow that mocked her with a grating caw.

Lila and Holly followed and swung wildly with their knives, knocking animals off Melody.

Xandie crouched next to Melody-bear. "Harrow House is warded so they can't get inside, but you need to change first before you can come in."

Lightning flashed overhead and this time struck a rotting falcon. With a sizzle, it dropped to the ground.

Melody shimmered and shrank down to her normal, overly large female form. Panting, the bear shifter rolled on to all fours and pushed herself up. "You Harrows are a menace. Freaky dead animals are stalking you, it's just wrong." She shuddered.

"Don't look at us. Even Holly wouldn't go near those disease-ridden things." Lila kicked a fox and squealed as her foot connected with a gooey squishing noise.

"We need to get inside now." Holly pointed to the ring of dead animals slowly closing in on the house.

"Right. That's enough of that." Elspeth jabbed

her sword into the ground in front of the porch and bellowed. Her voice, surprisingly loud for an elderly woman, caused light to flash out from around her body in an increasing arc of yellow light. Animal shrieks and moans filled the air, as they dropped to the ground, lifeless. Elspeth dusted her hands. "Ha. What did I tell you? No one wins against a Harrow."

Xandie watched in horror as another wave of larger animals stepped out from the wooded area at the side of Harrow House. "I think we have a problem."

"Hecate's toenails." Elspeth gathered up her sword again.

Melody stepped up next to Xandie and cracked her neck, before extending her hands and lengthening her nails until they resembled brightly decorated bear claws. "Are we going to talk about why you have angelic halos?"

"Elspeth," was Xandie's one-word answer.

Holly ran past screeching, a zombie owl attached to her hair. "Xandie, help me," she wailed as the owl dug in.

Raising her zombie-dicing knife, Xandie hollered back, "Stay still, so I can get a good swing up."

Holly froze and looked on in horror as Xandie swung her knife, dislodging the owl and slicing his wing off. Holly slumped. "Thank you. This is worse than the walking dead dragon at the funeral home."

Xandie grimaced and slowly inched away from Holly. "You might want to walk this way."

"Why?" Holly shifted wild eyes and slowly stared over her shoulder. A parade of zombie squirrels marched in unison straight at her. She squealed and dodged to the side, but the squirrels had her in their sights and ducked with her. They swarmed her feet, and a few clung on to her legs. "Xandie," she screeched.

Xandie raised her knife again. For some reason, those squirrels were homing in on Holly. She squinted at the zombie animals massing around her cousin. They weren't attacking her, they were... *licking her?* Writhing on her leg? Xandie gagged as she realized the plague of dead squirrels wanted some loving off her cousin. They didn't get the killer's memo of take down the Harrows. Instead, it was make love, not war.

"Help me." Holly stood on one leg, trying to shake the squirrels off her. A horrified expression bloomed on her face as she realized just what the dead animals' intentions were. *"Noooo."*

"Looks like one of us is getting lucky." Lila swung at a chittering zombie chipmunk. "I keep telling her about the mortuary stench she has going on. Those zombified critters love her."

"Lila Harrow, if you don't save me, I will get Elspeth to curse you," Holly screamed at her snickering cousin.

"This is one of those days I'd kill to have my camera on me. This would be great for blackmail." Lila moved toward Holly, knife raised.

"Why is it, if there's any trouble, there's always a Harrow in the thick of it?" Buchanan stepped around the side of the house with a pack of leather-jacketed Paladins, all with sharp swords in tow.

Lila whooped and jabbed her knife in the air, saving Holly forgotten. "Wahoo. Take that, walking dead. We have our own hunky reinforcements."

Melody whistled and plumped her brown hair. "A posse of leather-clad Paladins is nothing to sneer at. I may forgive you Harrows yet for my trauma."

Buchanan gestured to Holly, and his Paladins surged forward, swords gleaming in the light Elspeth had ramped up. They quickly dispatched the furry ankle lovers from my cousin.

She sagged against a hunky agent. "You just saved me from a fate worse than death." Holly patted his muscled chest. "Don't suppose you happen to be single and looking for some mayhem?"

Lila rolled her eyes. "In the middle of a zombie apocalypse and she's hitting on a squirrel slayer? Way to step out of her quiet shell. She gets all the breaks." Lila jabbed her knife into a stray furry body and pouted.

Buchanan stood toe to toe with Elspeth. "Will you admit you need help now?"

"I. Do. Not. Need. Paladin. Help," Elspeth hissed through her teeth at the aging man.

"Look around, old woman. Dead animals are stalking you. You're a target. We can help."

Elspeth picked her sword up and flung it into the air, skewering a blind horned owl against a tree. "I can help myself. Paladins only complicate things."

"It isn't just you, Elspeth." Buchanan nodded to Xandie and her cousins, along with Melody, all frantically swinging knives and claws.

Elspeth sagged. "Protect the girls. They're the ones who need it."

"We'll talk about the use of halos later, Elspeth," the Paladin warned the Harrow witch.

She ignored Buchanan and stomped off in another direction.

Xandie worked her way over to her grandmother, slicing and dicing as she went. "How did Buchanan know we needed help?" she yelled at Elspeth.

"Probably had one of you girls tagged for monitoring. Seems like something he'd do." Elspeth shrugged.

A police cruiser, with a host of other cars behind it, screamed up the driveway and slid to a stop, gravel spraying everyone.

Chief Braun and Agent Jackson tumbled out of their cars, weapons drawn, deputies and agents in tow. Braun and Jackson worked together, taking out animal after dead animal.

Without warning, all the remaining animals quivered and stiffened. Taking advantage of their pause, the Paladins shot relentlessly until every animal lay dead again.

Covered in gunk and panting, Xandie stepped up to her grandmother. "No more secrets, Elspeth. Someone wanted you dead or at least pinned down in Harrow House. Who do you know who could have done this?"

Elspeth dropped her sword at her feet and surveyed Harrow lands desecrated by dead animals. "Only one coven member ever had the power to raise that many dead at once."

Braun, Buchanan, and Jackson joined Xandie, listening intently to Elspeth's words.

"Hellacious Whitburn is the only Morrigan Coven member who could do this."

"And he's missing." Buchanan frowned, considering Elspeth.

"Is he? Or does he just want us to think that?" Xandie shook her head. Considering the surrounding devastation, things weren't looking good for Elspeth and Harrow House. Xandie needed to protect her family and find a killer. Hellacious Whitburn had become her number one suspect.

Now she just needed to hunt the missing necromancer down.

SEVEN

"Hellacious Whitburn wants you dead." Buchanan glared at Elspeth.

The old witch slapped the table and cackled. Lights and power fizzled in the bakery. "Hell will just have to get in line. There's a list a mile long of people who want me dead."

"Elspeth," Lila bellowed from her bakery kitchen. "I'm trying to bake here. Cut the evil witch routine if you want to eat."

Xandie covered her snicker with a cough. Elspeth had dolled herself up for this gathering of law enforcement, PIGs, Paladins, and Harrows. Her grandmother had donned a rainbow-colored, shoul-der-length wig and paired it with a watermelon-inspired pantsuit. Anyone would think she was trying to impress someone. And since Buchanan was the only person in the room old enough to date Elspeth...

Elspeth narrowed her gaze at Xandie. "It's true. My enemies are plentiful."

Xandie held a hand up in surrender. "No argument here."

Agent Jackson stepped forward. "We have a current list of five names with a serious axe to grind. And a further twenty also unhappy with Elspeth. Your former co-worker, Hellacious Whitburn, tops the list. But we still need to narrow the suspect pool."

Elspeth sniffed and then dropped below the table. Rummaging noises came from underneath, along with a victorious holler from Elspeth as she popped back up with her bedazzled hipflask. She tipped a salute to Aggie Braun before guzzling a large mouthful of liquid.

Jackson quirked an eyebrow at Aggie. "The chain of custody for crime scene evidence isn't a concern for Point Muse law enforcement?"

Aggie snorted. "Please, it's obvious the killer isn't Elspeth. If it was, no one would find a body, let alone a flask, with or without her name bedazzled on it. This was planted at the scene by an idiot, clearly."

Zach patted his mother on her large shoulder

before sneering at the Paranormal Investigative Group agent. "We've done our due diligence and eliminated Elspeth Harrow from our suspect pool. No reason she couldn't have her hipflask back. Now, how about you do some heavy lifting instead of leaving it up to Paladin Inc. and Point Muse law enforcement?"

Xandie watched transfixed as Zach's ice-blue eyes flashed silver and his frame grew until he towered over the PIG agent. She still hadn't sorted out exactly how she felt about Jackson wiping her memory back in Andrews, her old hometown. She only knew she was angry about his interference and that wouldn't change any time soon. But Point Muse had become home, and she just hated to admit his high-handed actions were justified.

An unruffled Ethan Jackson stepped up to Zach and grinned, teeth gleaming white. "Far be it from me, Braun, to expect professionalism. If you've got something to say, *Leo,* spit it out."

Oh yeah. Forget-Me-Witch Jackson isn't happy either and neither is he backing down. Xandie prepared for an alpha male fight for supremacy. She wasn't entirely sure who she wanted to win.

Buchanan thumped his hand down on the table next to Elspeth. "Put your alphas away, boys. This is a joint task force which Paladin Inc. is spearheading. Basically, you do what *I* say."

Aggie pushed herself between the shifter and the witch and gave them each a good shove. "Plus, if you don't stop posturing, Elspeth will hex you so every food you eat tastes like poop. So, back the heckadoodle down, kids."

Taking heed of Aggie's warning, the rival law enforcement officers stepped apart and proceeded to ignore each other.

Xandie bit her lip, amusement bubbling up. Jackson was tall with a swimmer's body, wide shoulders, and a tiny waist. His brown hair curled around the collar of a smart navy suit. In direct contrast to Zach Braun's bear shifter body, whose large muscled shoulders slid into a solid waist and heavy thighs. He balanced, ready for action, in his trim black police uniform. His sandy brown, non-regulation haircut that flopped over his forehead did little to hide the scorn in his eyes. Different men, but the same masculine urge to challenge each other.

Xandie added in her contribution to the conversation flowing around her. "Whitburn's a necromancer, and dead animals attacked Harrow House last night. I'm sure that's called a clue."

"Alexandra is right. Whitburn is our focus. He's

got to be in the area." Buchanan pointed to Jackson and Braun. "Get state and local eyes on him. I want to know where he is and his every move before he disappears again."

Buchanan turned to Elspeth and growled, "You need to give everyone a rundown on Morrigan again and the Morpheus Amulet, but nothing gets repeated outside the bakery. Got it?" Buchanan eyeballed the agents in the room and then pointed a finger at Elspeth. "Speak, witch, and make it snappy."

Elspeth shot Buchanan a look that promised retribution later but honored his request. "Most of you know PIG formed the Morrigan Coven to stop Hitler's use of certain artifacts and his encroachment into the supernatural world. It was nominally under Paranormal Investigative Group special projects but was pretty much autonomous. Head of the Department was Albert Proctor. The donkey's behind." Elspeth's face soured as she sipped from her flask, the diamonds catching the light and throwing sparkled flashes onto the walls.

"PIG recruited members from different supernatural groups. Minerva Crow was a shifter, Henry Strongarm was a descendant of Hercules, and Hellacious Whitburn was a necromancer. I was a hexer and caster, Bridget Doyle a seer, and Lucien Benoit was a vampire. Albert Proctor oversaw us, and Hannah Lynch was his intern and admin."

Lila deposited a large plate of blueberry muffins on the table before slinking back to the kitchen.

Elspeth paused while everyone dug in. "In the beginning, it worked. We stemmed the tide of artifacts flowing into Hitler's sweaty little hands. Hellacious turned double agent and went undercover with Hitler as his artifact expert, and no one suspected him. But the war rolled on, and Hitler's obsession with the supernatural worsened. Proctor ordered the coven to step up our artifact retrieval. The end justified any means to break Hitler's grasp on the world."

Elspeth shook her head and was silent for a few moments. Then she continued, her voice raspy with remembered pain. "Because of our experience with artifacts and their use, they tasked us to start interacting within certain fieldwork parameters. I noticed small things at first. Minor changes to duty rosters, contact locations altered, artifact disposal routines changed. Then Proctor upped our quota of artifacts. The smaller, less notable artifacts disappeared from our inventories. At the same time, our mission parameters were becoming more fluid, less rigid. Proctor didn't care how we achieved our missions. Or who was hurt." Elspeth gripped her flask tight, knuckles and fingers ivory against the bedazzled pink.

Xandie stepped around an agent, planning to stand by her grandmother's side, but Buchanan was there before her, his hand resting on the elderly woman's shoulder.

"I knew Proctor was on the take, but no one believed me. Not even my coven members. In fact, they turned on me." Elspeth glared at Agent Jackson. "Neither PIG nor the coven bothered to investigate, and Proctor kept stealing, but the artifacts weren't insignificant anymore. He was targeting more and more dangerous and larger artifacts. I was coven head, but I was being cut out of the loop on almost every mission. Hannah Lynch, our intern, stopped briefing me, and that was the last straw. I contacted Paladin Inc. They immediately assigned a handler to investigate my claims."

"Grandfather," Xandie murmured.

Elspeth nodded, her eyes glimmering before she blinked the memories away. "He was an obnoxious do-gooder, but he was a hottie and he listened. Lucas agreed with me, and I went back to the coven as an informant. I found evidence of Proctor's dealings and the fact Whitburn was his dealer to the black witch market. Proctor became obsessed with the

Morpheus Amulet, and the coven's body count of collateral damage escalated. Hitler deployed the amulet in Poland but only focused on certain supernatural groups. It was a slaughter."

"If Proctor was so corrupted, why didn't anyone else see?" Xandie couldn't fathom the fact that someone could get away with this magnitude of dodgy dealings. Well...*except for Elspeth.*

"The threat of Hitler overwhelmed everything. People were so tunnel-visioned on the evil he presented, they couldn't see others taking advantage of the situation. Proctor ordered all our other missions shelved, and our sole focus became the amulet. We snagged it, but Proctor disappeared and took the amulet with him. Lucas and I tracked him down. We used a bait and switch with a fake amulet. He was so far off the rails by then that when he realized what had happened, he deployed an absorber hex. He sucked in all the electricity in the area and then just exploded. Not long after that, Hitler died, and the coven disbanded. They hated me. None of them forgave me for what they considered was my betrayal. We split up the amulet. I had a piece, but so did Henry, Doyle, and Lucien."

Xandie frowned. "What about Whitburn and Hannah Lynch? Did they get a piece as well?"

Elspeth shook her head. "Hell knew PIG would bust him for dealing in Proctor's dirty artifacts scheme. He disappeared before Morrigan disbanded. No one heard from him for years, until he sprang up in Silicon Valley in the eighties and nineties with his necromantic game and made millions."

"And Hannah?" Braun leaned forward, hooked by Elspeth's tale.

"Hannah was a complete null. No magic worked against her. She ate it up and magic disappeared, a complete black hole. It devastated her when Proctor's dirty dealings came to light. Hannah idolized him. She wanted nothing to do with the amulet and returned to admin at PIG."

Buchanan dropped his hand from Elspeth's shoulder. "Hannah died in a car bomb, but we found traces of magical accelerant. Some kind of fire hex."

Elspeth continued with fists clenched. "Lucas and I settled in Point Muse and had a family. Five years later, Lucas was called into a high-level Paladin meeting in Boston. Some kid crashed the meeting and used the same absorber hex that killed Proctor to blow the Headquarters to pieces. No survivors. The kid was Edwin Proctor, Albert Proctor's only child. He was nineteen years old."

Xandie covered her gasp with a hand over her

mouth. No wonder her grandmother was the suspicious, sarcastic, devious woman she was. To go through all she had would have broken a weaker woman.

"That's why Paladin ordered me to do protective detail. We protect our own and whether or not Elspeth wants to admit it, she's Paladin family. I'm moving into Harrow House, and I'll set up a protective and surveillance detail as well." Buchanan braced against the table.

Elspeth exploded out of her chair as fast as an octogenarian could. "Nope. No way. Paladin can stick their protective detail up their..."

"Now, Elspeth. Take a breath before you say something you regret." Aggie stepped forward, hands outstretched.

Elspeth shuffled back from her friend and spun on Buchanan. "You," she intoned dramatically. "You planned this, didn't you? You've always been hot for this sugar momma." Elspeth shimmied her hips and glared at the room, daring anyone to speak.

Deciding retreat was the best option, Xandie sidled back and made a dash for the kitchen. She swung the door open and knocked Lila to the floor.

"Geez, be more careful of eavesdroppers." Lila

rubbed a red lump in the middle of her forehead and then hauled herself upright.

"Did you hear everything?" Xandie propped herself against the kitchen counter and stole a chocolate muffin, still steaming hot, out of the muffin tray.

"Yeah, even down to the hot body comment." Lila shuddered. "I'm betting Elspeth shimmied too. So glad I missed that."

Xandie swallowed a mouthful. "Kind of explains Elspeth though, doesn't it? Should have guessed she'd have a secret spy past."

Lila busied herself cleaning counters and emptying garbage into a trashcan. She shoved it at Xandie. "You can pay for your thieving of my baked goods by taking the trash out." Lila jerked her head at the alley behind her shop.

"Fine." Xandie grabbed the trash bag and slid out the door into the alley, almost stumbling over a brassy blonde waitress puffing on a cigarette.

"I'm so sorry." Xandie dumped the bag and reached out a hand to the woman sprawled on the ground. "I have a habit of leaping before I look."

Using Xandie's hand, the server hauled herself up and smiled. "No worries, ducky. I should have looked where I was standing." The woman, somewhere in her late fifties, patted her brassy blonde hair and adjusted her tight top. "I'm Delilah. I work at Heaven's Diner." She pointed toward the end of the alley. "I smoke out here so the boss doesn't complain. Reformed ex-smokers are horrible to work for." She rolled her heavily made-up green eyes.

"I'm Xandie Meyers." She held out a hand again and gingerly shook Delilah's red-taloned fingers.

"You're the new Librarian. My parents used to drive through here and consult the Library all the time." Delilah giggled. "My dad was a weather mage and always made sure he and Mom got snowed in here so they could spend extra time in the Library."

Nice that someone had a good opinion of the Library and Point Muse. With all the bodies turning up, you'd think they were the murder capital of Maine. "Are you a weather mage?"

"Lordy, no." Delilah belly-laughed at the idea. "I'm more of a good luck charm. Things just turn out right for me. You know?"

"Not really. I'm the Librarian, so luck isn't really my thing."

Delilah flicked out the hot part of her cigarette and then shoved the butt in the pocket of her uniform. "Well, better get back before the boss loses it. If you want something to eat, come on in. The food's great." She waved and wobbled off in her not-so-practical wedge sandals.

Xandie smiled at the sight of the waitress. Big, brassy blonde hair, tight uniform, wedge sandals, and sharp red nails presented an image of a man-eater. But Delilah came across as warm and welcoming. Maybe Xandie *should* pop into the diner for lunch?

The sound of shattering glass and Elspeth's high-pitched shrieks made her decision. Lunch, Delilah, and an Elspeth-free zone was her priority for the day.

The second was tracking down a killer with a grudge.

EIGHT

"And *I* said over my dead body." Elspeth slapped the diner tabletop.

"Remind me again why we had to bring Elspeth?" Holly leaned over and murmured in Xandie's ear.

"Because she's possibly targeted for death by a crazy killer, and she's our grandmother," Xandie whispered back.

"I can hear you," Elspeth sang, but her melody was threatening. "Where is that waitress? The lobster pie is calling my name."

"So is indigestion." Xandie had thought she'd sneak away for lunch, but Elspeth had eagled-eyed her as soon as she'd snuck into Lila's bakery. She'd wound up agreeing to take Elspeth to lunch to keep an eye on her. Privately, she had a feeling Buchanan was taking up occupancy in Harrow House while Elspeth was out of the way. Made it harder to evict him when her grandmother eventually discovered him.

"Delilah, customers," a tattoo-covered bald man yelled from the kitchen.

"I hear ya." Delilah rushed out, notepad at the ready. She stopped short when she spotted Xandie and the Harrows before continuing to the table with an overly wide smile. "Hello there. You decided to get lunch and brought some friends?"

"Hi, Delilah. This is my grandmother, Elspeth, and my cousin, Holly." Xandie waved a hand at her family.

Delilah nodded, her gaze traveling over the Harrows, snagging for a minute on Elspeth before moving on. "Nice to see you here. So, what can I get you?"

Elspeth dropped the menu onto the table. "Lobster pie and a double shot cappuccino for me."

Xandie butted in. "Change the coffee to a ginger ale, please. Last thing we need is Elspeth caffeinated."

"I *am* an adult." Elspeth glowered at her granddaughter.

"An adult in no need of a double shot caffeine hit when she has a hipflask filled with goodness knows what." Elspeth, au natural, was hard enough to deal with, let alone a caffeine fueled one.

"Fine." Elspeth sneered the word and slumped in the booth seat. Drumming her fingers, she ignored everyone, surly like an eight-year-old rather than eighty-something-year-old.

Holly smiled at Delilah. "A lobster burger for me, please."

Delilah scribbled on her notepad and then turned her smile on Xandie. "What about you, sweetie?"

"Blueberry pancakes, please."

Delilah gathered up the menus. "Food coming up soon. I'll bring some water over in a minute." With a wave, Delilah headed to the kitchen.

"Who won the fight? Buchanan or Elspeth?" Holly quirked an eyebrow at Elspeth. "I wouldn't mind Buchanan moving in if he brings some hunkie Paladin agents with him."

Elspeth snorted. "You'll never snag a husband if you throw yourself at men like your cousin Lila."

Holly rolled her eyes. "Who said anything about a husband? That PIG agent isn't bad either."

"That memory-stealing, slithering skunk of a law

enforcement agent can stay out of my way." Xandie played with a saltshaker. The damn man annoyed her with his high-handed thievery of her memories of Andrews College and the pixie murder. Not to mention his magically interfering nudge to visit Point Muse for answers. No one likes their actions controlled by another. Especially not a Harrow.

"Be more like Xandie. She has multiple choices of men. Even if they *are* both law enforcement." Elspeth fake retched in disgust and then took a chug from her flask. "Then again, that morgue odor is a turnoff."

"Why, you old..."

Delilah interrupted Holly's tirade with a carafe of water and three glasses. "Food will be out in a minute. I couldn't help but hear you mention the Paranormal Investigative Group? Between them and the Paladin guys, it's an eye-catching feast." Delilah winked. "Any idea why they're all here?" She snapped her fingers. "Hey, it isn't because of the murder of that teacher guy, is it?"

Elspeth glared suspiciously at Delilah. "How's our food coming along? On a timetable, you know. A dose of prune juice is calling."

Delilah sniffed. "I'll check on your meals."

Xandie watched the now miffed waitress disappear into the kitchen again. "Great, Elspeth. They'll probably spit in our food now. Ever heard of tact?"

"Tact is for those do-gooder Paladins. I'm all about action."

"Speaking of action, how come you never told us about the Morrigan Coven?"

"None of your business, Death Girl." Elspeth sniffed disdain at Holly's question.

"It sort of is now. Since I live in the same house and I'm as much of a target as you." Holly exchanged dueling glares with her grandmother.

Xandie sighed in relief as Delilah marched up without a smile and dumped their plates in front of them.

Distracted by food, Elspeth ignored her grand-daughters and dug in.

Still holding a grudge, Holly scowled at Elspeth. "We'll nose out your secrets, old woman. You haven't outwitted us yet."

"Well, well. What a surprise to see a Harrow annoying people. She has a talent for giving people indigestion." A short, plump, graying redhead stood with gloved hands on her hips.

Elspeth spat her mouthful of food onto her plate and thumped her chest. "See, told you someone was trying to murder me. I nearly choked to death."

"Ha, you're too ornery to die," the woman screeched.

"Wow, Elspeth. Way to make friends." Xandie offered a hand and a smile to the stranger. "Hi, I'm Xandie Meyers, Elspeth's granddaughter, and this is my cousin, Holly."

The old woman ignored Xandie's outstretched hand but offered a saccharine sweet smile. "My commiserations on being stuck with Elspeth as a grandmother. I'm Bridget Doyle. I used to work with that viper." She pointed to Elspeth.

"Ha." Elspeth shoved her lobster pie away. "You call it working, I call it playing with forces you don't understand."

"Please, we were equal. We all agreed on our mission parameters. You're the one who took it outside of the coven and look at what that caused."

Both women were breathing heavily, red cheeks flaring. This was obviously an old argument a chance meeting in a diner wouldn't solve. *But was it chance?* "You're a Morrigan Coven member?" Xandie raised an eyebrow in question.

"And proud of it." Bridget Doyle straightened and puffed her chest out. Her narrowed glare dared Elspeth to comment.

"And now it's going to kill us." Elspeth stood abruptly and shoved past her old coven member.

"I've got her." Holly threw some money on the table and followed behind her grandmother as she stomped out.

Xandie smiled weakly at Elspeth's nemesis. "Sorry. With all the murder, she's under a lot of stress."

Bridget nodded, her face sad. "Henry was a lovely man, and Minerva and Elspeth were thick as thieves once. Elspeth never really believed in what we were doing. I guess she got what she wanted in the end."

"Maybe, but the end doesn't always justify the means."

"You sound like your grandmother. *And* your grandfather, come to think of it."

"That's mean." Xandie smiled to show she was joking and stood. "It was nice meeting you." She reached out and shook Bridget's hand.

Bridget jerked with a hiss and cradled her gloved hand close to her chest.

"Sorry, did I hurt you?" *Talk about an extreme reaction.*

Bridget let out a jagged breath and smiled through watery eyes. "Sorry. I got a bit of a shock.

I'm a seer, so I wear gloves everywhere, and I don't touch strangers. Nothing like shaking someone's hand and seeing their life and death."

Xandie grimaced. "Apologies again. But except for a few dead bodies, my life's pretty boring."

Bridget shook head. "You don't understand. I jerked because you're blank. Nothing. I've only ever come across a few others like that. Nulls, null space magic users."

Interesting. Must be the Library's protections. "Would one of those people be Hannah Lynch?"

"Obviously, Elspeth shared something of the coven, but yes, you're right. Hannah was a null. It ran in her family, apparently. I couldn't read anything from her. Or anything from our old boss, Proctor, either. I think he had protective amulets, so no one could read him."

Xandie spotted movement out of the corner of her eye, but when she spun about, no one was there. Dismissing it, she turned back to Bridget. "A shame you couldn't have read him, but I guess life doesn't roll out page by page."

Bridget offered a tight smile. "I didn't suspect Proctor, but still, I was just as deceived and angry as Elspeth was when we all found out. Poor Hannah was the most shattered of all of us. She idolized the man."

"And now someone's killing members and stealing amulet pieces."

"I'm pretty sure I'll see the murderer coming." Bridget smirked, confident in her ability to outsmart the killer.

"Any clue who's targeting your coven?"

Bridget pointed an accusing finger at the still squabbling duo of Elspeth and Holly.

"Elspeth target her old friends?" Xandie scoffed. "If Elspeth killed someone, do you really think we'd even see a body? She's too devious to get caught."

"She *is* devious," Bridget allowed. "And she collects enemies. If it isn't her, it could be any of several villains."

"I heard that Morrigan ruffled a few feathers too in their collection of artifacts."

"A possibility. But I'm still safe from the likes of murderous killers."

The doorbell jangled behind Xandie, and she stepped aside as two Paladin agents stepped in.

"Delilah. Customers, girl," the owner bellowed. "Delilah, where the dang are you?" Giving up, he appeared behind the counter to serve.

"I hope you're right. For your sake. If you need help, we're at Harrow House." Xandie nodded to Elspeth's nemesis and strode out to join her cackling witch of a grandmother and no doubt a frazzled Holly. Speaking to Bridget raised more questions. She hoped she could answer some of them before they found another corpse.

NINE

"Is it dead?" Xandie poked the limp rat with a broom.

"I work at a funeral home. Yes, it's dead."

"Kind of sad. Come in for some milk and head out on a stretcher." Lila wiped a stray tear away.

"It's a rat." Holly bit the words out.

"So casual about death, cousin. The funeral home has changed you." Lila shook her head sadly.

"For death's sake, can we just move the rat outside and get on with eating pizza? I am so sick of being surrounded by reanimated animals that haven't had decent burial rituals performed. It's damaging my psyche."

Xandie stifled an inappropriate giggle at Holly's words. If her cousins were warring, she couldn't show humor to any side. Both the Harrows held grudges for a long time. She was grateful that she'd left Elspeth at home, exhausted from fighting with Buchanan. When their grandmother decided to have an early night, the girls voted to grab some groceries and get a pizza. Otherwise, Elspeth would've been in the thick of the squabbling, enjoying the chaos, provoking and poking.

"I'm so sorry, ladies. This has never happened before." The leprechaun owner of Eat Right Grocery Store rubbed his hands together.

"Having rats or them dying in the middle of our milk delivery?"

"Both," he burst out. "My regular driver didn't turn up because he won some cruise, and then the new guy spills your delivery and disappears."

Cruise? Sounded just like her aunts, Amelia and Winifred, and Colin the pug, on their cruise. "Did your old driver tell you anything else about the cruise he won?"

"That he was contacted out of the blue. Doesn't even remember entering the competition. But he won a two-week supernatural singles' cruise. All he had to do was pick the tickets up from the office of the cruise company ASAP. They were left under some woman's name. That's all I remember."

Exactly the same as her aunt's prize-winning cruise tickets. "And your new guy?"

"Popped up the same day my regular guy left. Asked for a job. I hired him on the spot. He was doing okay until this morning."

Until Harrow House's milk run. "He was getting the Harrow order ready, then what?"

The leprechaun nodded at the agent stationed at the front entrance. "My guy was getting the order ready. He popped his head out to speak to me and saw the agent come in. Next thing I knew, there was an enormous crash and he split. No sign of him, just a dead rat in the middle of the milk."

The same milk her grandmother guzzled every morning in a smoothie concoction.

"Find a dead body and Xandie Meyers is in the same room." Agent Ethan Jackson leaned against the doorjamb of the stock room, his mouth turned up in a grin that could melt most women into a puddle. *Most* women.

Holly giggled like a little girl. "Just call the Harrows death magnets. What can we do for you, Agent Jackson?"

"Please, call me Ethan." He bowed with a deep flourish, causing Lila to snort.

"I'm sure that rat doesn't need a Paranormal

Investigative Group agent poking his nose into Harrow business." Xandie folded her arms over her chest and glared.

"It does when a rat is dead in the Harrow milk delivery." Ethan knelt and, using his wand, turned the dead rat over. He poked at the milk container and exposed a tiny hole in the carton. "Looks like it nibbled its way in and drank some of the milk. Judging by the blisters around his mouth, I'd say Toxicodendron Radicans."

"Huh?" Poisons were not her core interest. Jackson might as well be speaking gibberish to Xandie.

"Poison ivy." Lila shuddered. "I had a run-in when I was a teenager. It was traumatizing."

"You were making out with Bronson, Cupid's grandson, so it serves you right." Holly sniffed in disgust.

Lila waved her hands like a wild woman. "Argh. How many times do I have to explain? I had no clue you liked him. Besides, he jabbed me with his arrow. What was I supposed to do?"

Xandie grimaced. That picture would last a lifetime. "But poison ivy doesn't kill. You just get itchy and grow blisters, right?"

Jackson wiped his wand off on a rag and stood.

"Normally, over a week, you get rashes, blisters. Severe cases can even affect airways, but the killer paired the poison with an elemental hex. That would have beefed up the earth magic of the plant and boosted the poison. Toxicity and death would happen quickly."

"And if Elspeth had drunk a poison ivy-laced smoothie tomorrow morning when she woke up?" First the reanimated animal corpses, and now this. Xandie had better find the damn killer as fast as she could, otherwise she'd be eulogizing at Elspeth's funeral.

"Probably not enough to kill. But it would make her very sick." Jackson whipped out a black bag and scooped the rat up. He threw it at the Paladin agent. "Catch. I'm betting Buchanan will want to have a look at that."

The agent snatched the bag out of the air. "I'll notify Chief Braun and get the crime scene sealed off."

Jackson nodded in agreement and focused on the girls. "I'd suggest you head home and keep an eye on Elspeth instead of engaging in a night on the town."

"Pizza does not equal a hot night out, but we get your message." Xandie gritted her teeth but agreed with the pain-in-the-neck agent.

Lila grabbed Holly and whipped out her keys. "We can nuke the pizza when we get back. I'll drive."

"Don't you have an apartment to go to?" Holly grumbled.

"Yeah, but Harrow House has leather-clad hotties guarding Harrow blood." She grinned when her cousin shot out the door. Lila waved to Xandie as she scooted after Holly.

"I can drop you home. You don't have to walk in the dark," Jackson offered to Xandie.

"Fine. But I still haven't forgiven you for wiping my memory."

Jackson led the way outside to a plain unmarked car. "If it's any consolation, you're the only person who has ever recovered memories after a wipe."

"Nope, no consolation."

A patrol car driven by Chief Braun pulled into the grocery store parking lot as Jackson drove out.

"Should we stop for Braun and update him?"

"Considering the recent Paladin-Point Muse Police Department alliance, the agent can update Chief Braun sufficiently. If he wants more information, he can hunt one of us down." Ethan pulled out onto the road but pointed at the area near Xandie's feet. "Have a look."

Confused, Xandie reached down and pulled a couple of files out. "What are these?"

"One is your grandmother's file. The other is what we have on Hellacious Whitburn."

Giving into her curiosity, Xandie opened the file on her grandmother. "Top secret classified?"

"It was a special access program during World War Two. They were pretty much off the books. Minimal records. Field agents made up their own rules. As long as the missions were completed, the powers-that-be didn't care about administration practices."

Xandie scanned the file. The first page was Elspeth's statistics. Age, weight, and aliases. Elspeth had an alias? "What's a caster witch?"

"Means Elspeth can cast without a circle, ritual, or spell ingredient. But her specialty is hexes. Detecting and casting them. Elspeth is powerful, dangerous, and erratic. Keep reading." Ethan never took his eyes off the road as he navigated downtown Point Muse.

Xandie flicked through the pages detailing Elspeth's antics. Most had black redacted boxes covering names and people. Albert Proctor's name, however, caught Xandie's attention, and she slipped out the report. "'*Elspeth Harrow is a highly skilled caster witch, blinded by her self-importance*'?"

Jackson coughed. "Proctor wasn't impressed by your grandmother. His reports are pretty scathing."

"'*Paranoid delusions, obsession with procuring magical artifacts. Flouts authority and ignores instructions.*' Yep, he hated her." Shame he'd died. Proctor would've been Xandie's number one suspect.

"Remember, Elspeth suspected him of acquiring and selling black magic artifacts. They detested each other."

"PIG should have listened to her."

"I think the evidence warranted a more thorough investigation than what occurred." He shrugged. "But things have changed since then."

Xandie slipped out a single piece of parchment hidden at the bottom of the pile. She looked up at Ethan in shock. "My grandfather?"

"Once Paladin decided Proctor was an Armageddon risk, they assigned a handler for Elspeth. That was your grandfather."

Lucas Munro's report was the direct opposite to Proctor's. It detailed misappropriation, mishandling and negligent activities carried out by the Morrigan Coven. His recommendation was for Elspeth Harrow to go undercover to expose Proctor's abuse of power. "He had faith in her and what she'd uncovered. No wonder she fell for him."

Jackson snorted as he pulled into Xandie's drive. Lights immediately blazed on in the Library. "Braver man than I am to take on a Harrow witch."

Xandie snapped the file at the agent. "You'll never get a chance to know, memory thief."

He grabbed the weaponized file from Xandie and dropped it on the seat behind him. "You'll never let go of that, will you? Did you ever think I wouldn't have been able to do it if the Library hadn't wanted me to?"

"Don't. Remind. Me." Realistically, she understood why he'd had to do it, and the Library had agreed to it. It protected her from all magic, except that which it deemed necessary. But it still annoyed her.

Ethan tendered Xandie a charming smile. "Fancy a coffee nightcap? We can go over the files again?"

Xandie had seen both the Proctor and Elspeth files. Now she wanted to know one thing from agent Ethan Jackson. "You have a file on my grandmother and my grandfather. What about me? Xandie Meyers?"

He looked uncomfortable. "Anyone who has the potential to be a threat has a file."

Xandie raised both eyebrows. "Not exactly an answer. Or is it? So, I'm a threat? Is that what you're saying?"

Jackson tapped the steering wheel. "You're the Librarian to the Great Supernatural Library of Alexandria. You could interfere and control any aspect of the hidden world. Yes, you have a file."

He thought she was a threat? That she could stoop so low as to manipulate her connection to the Library? He didn't know the real her. Xandie snatched the file on Whitburn, opened the car door, and slammed it behind her. She'd read the file in peace after cleaning up the Library.

Jackson yelled through the open driver's window, "I take it the nightcap is off?"

Xandie opened her front door before turning to face Jackson. "I'd hate for you to feel uncomfortable having coffee with a potential global threat to the world." With that, she slammed the door shut. The resounding thump echoed her satisfaction at having the last word.

TEN

"Of course the guy has a file on you. You're the Librarian with access to potentially life-destroying power." Theo licked his pet imp, Horatio, soaking the hairless imp's hot-pink tracksuit.

Xandie growled and shelved a title on *Unicorn Slaying Procedures*. "I am not a security risk. That's Elspeth, not me."

Theo coughed up a furball, narrowly avoiding the imp. "That's all Harrow witches."

She had to admit, Harrow women thrived on chaos and mayhem. Especially Elspeth. Her cousin, Holly, was the only exception to the rule. The banshee always seemed to have a little pocket of serenity around her. Except when she squabbled with their cousin, Lila. Then fireworks detonated her aura of peace. "I still don't like the idea." Xandie whined her complaint and then exhaled. "I guess I can understand why, but it still annoys me." She narrowed her gaze and glared around. "And I haven't forgotten your role in this, Library."

The lights in the circular room flickered a little, as if in regret.

"I still love you, but I'm not happy with your actions, got it?" The Library lights blazed bright before settling to a warm glow. A flotilla of flying scrolls lifted into the air and dueled madly above Xandie. A swirling whirligig of white notes drifted down around her like large paper snowflakes.

Xandie snagged the scrolls and unrolled one tied off with a red ribbon and read out loud, *"Vampire— Blunt Instrument or Quasi Souled Entity?"* Many weird and wonderful writings made it into the Library. Curiosity had Xandie unrolling two other scrolls. *"The Care and Handling of Wounded Vampires. How to Cultivate a Vampire: Make Allies, not Enemies."*

Xandie dropped the scrolls into the shelving bin. "Vampires on the brain, Library?" Not expecting an answer, she tackled all the notes. Every time the Library granted an information or access request, a small note was generated and delivered to Xandie for action. She'd write an appointment in the diary, and the Library would decide if or when to issue an invitation.

"Have I been neglecting you lately? Is that why you've stored up all these requests?"

"I'd take those requests as a yes. You have been somewhat involved with finding dead bodies," Theo remarked snidely, ignoring the chittering Horatio.

"I'm a catalyst, remember, Theo? Just like my mother. Bodies find me, not the other way around. Actually..." Xandie tapped her chin. "Should I ask the Library about Morrigan again?"

"You've done that before and came up with bupkis. What makes now so different?"

"Because Jackson recently shared Elspeth and Whitburn's files with me." Maybe the Library would let her access information now? "Library? Could I have access to all Morrigan Coven information? The Paranormal Investigative Group has already shared files. Surely, I should have access?" Xandie flicked to a free page in the appointment book and read the words that formed. "*Access now marginal. Information pending.*" It was a start. She'd have to wait for the information to surface.

Xandie smiled her thanks and took a deep breath as she looked around. Every shelf gleamed, every book shelved in the correct place. Deep leather armchairs and low tables sat ready for use. Empty desks lined one end of the room and a fireplace, also clean, now graced the wall near the waiting room. "When did we get a fireplace?

"The same time the Library decided we need an antique Victorian fainting couch and a first aid kit. This morning."

"That's a tad ominous."

"Roll with the Library, Meyers." Theo stretched, his back arching. "I would suggest you leave Whitburn's file and the information the Library digs up until after you've waded through the Library requests. Otherwise, she'll think you're ignoring her."

Theo could have a point. Xandie collected the scattered notes and systematically waded through them. Some she wrote in the book and some she binned. Xandie was pretty sure needing a place for a make-out session did not qualify as Library business. One name caught Xandie's attention. "Lucien Benoit requested access? Where have I seen that name before?"

A book on vampire clans lifted into the air and landed in front of Xandie. She clicked her fingers. "The Library got it right. Benoit was a vampire and a coven member. According to Elspeth's files, he was a friend and accomplice of hers."

"What does the vampire look like?"

Xandie paged through the clan book until she found a description. "Ah, tall and skinny, with a sharp nose only a mother could love."

"And pale? Very, very pale?"

Xandie slammed the book shut. "He's a vampire. Of course he's pale."

"And at the window," Theo pointed out helpfully and backed away from the window.

Xandie spun to face the windows and screeched. A tall, pale man with a beak of a nose hugged the window, scratching at the glass.

"Library, we have an intruder," Theo hissed and gathered Horatio, depositing him on his back, both ready for a quick getaway.

The scratching vampire pushed himself away from the window and disappeared from view.

Xandie hefted the tome on vampire clans and raised it overhead. She took a cautious step to the window and peered out. It was fully dark, and barely any light cut the black night outside. "Where has he gone? I can't see anything?"

"Xandie?"

She continued to peer outside as she answered Theo, "What's up?"

"Did you lock the waiting room door?"

"Yes."

"What about the Library door?"

Xandie spun around. "I... maybe?"

"I think that maybe should have been a no." Theo pointed with a paw at the door that was slowly opening, one creak at a time.

"Library, it'd be great if you did something *right* now," Xandie hollered as she hoisted a book, ready to throw. The lights muted to a welcoming glow.

"Don't think the Library's worried, Xandie." Theo cowered under a leather armchair.

"Fine. I'll deal with this myself." Xandie threw the book as the door swung open, but it landed harmlessly on the floor.

"*Bonjour*, Librarian. I need some help." The tall, beaky nosed vampire stumbled into the room.

"We are not food and are armed with heavy books that hurt when thrown." Xandie hefted another book menacingly.

"Why on earth would I hurt the Librarian and a Harrow? Elspeth would have my non-beating heart in a moment." The vampire wavered, blinking glassy eyes. "I believe I'm going to pass out. Contact

Elspeth. She'll know what to do." With that, the vampire collapsed gracefully onto the fainting couch.

"So that's why the Library redecorated," Theo murmured as he crawled out from underneath the chair.

Xandie tentatively walked forward and poked the unconscious vampire. His chest rose and fell slowly—*very slowly*—but otherwise, he was out. Xandie noticed a red patch spreading on the flouncy white shirt. Lifting a torn edge, she peeked underneath and spotted a weeping tear in the left side of his chest. Xandie grabbed a wad of bandages, plugging the hole as well as she could. But she needed to do more. She just had no clue about vampire physiology. Xandie needed help. She needed Elspeth.

Xandie needed her grandmother, or she'd have another body on her hands.

Literally...

<hr>

"Aren't vampires supposed to explode if they go out during the day?" Xandie whispered to Lila as they watched Buchanan and Elspeth clean up after stitching Lucien Benoit's chest. She'd gotten a distress call out to Elspeth, and her grandmother had come racing to the Library with Buchanan and Lila's bakery van in tow. She'd performed a basic patch job on his wound and shifted him to Harrow House.

"The very skilled Elspeth dealt with that issue decades ago."

The thin tone of Lucien Benoit reached Xandie's ears. She fought the red wave threatening to cover her cheeks. "Sorry, I'm relatively new to all this supernatural stuff."

Lucien pushed himself up on the couch with a wince. He patted Elspeth's hands as she fussed around. "Enough, *ma petite*. I am whole, thanks to you. But your granddaughter needs to know all."

"Argh." Elspeth stomped off, swearing all the way.

Lucien smiled. "I adore my Elspeth, but she doesn't cope well when those she cares about are hurt or threatened."

"Who says I care about you, Benoit? You've always been a thorn in my side," Elspeth snapped.

"Ah, but I am also all that is debonair." The tall vampire winked at Holly and Lila.

"He was more a minion than a thorn. Elspeth was the ringleader and Minerva and Benoit, her loyal subjects. They thrived on the chaos she caused," Buchanan added in a dry tone.

"Elspeth, she was *magnifique* with mayhem." Benoit shook his head. "We should have believed her when she told us about Proctor, Whitburn, and the Morpheus Amulet. For that, my Elspeth, I am deeply sorry." He raised a shaking hand to his chest and rubbed it.

"Oh, for Hecate's sake." Elspeth stomped to Lucien and shoved a clear glass filled with bubbling purple liquid at him. "Drink this." She dangled the glass in front of Benoit and scowled until he drank. Then she turned to Xandie. "Thank you for calling us. He's always had a lousy sense of direction."

Swallowing manfully, Lucien shook his finger at Elspeth playfully. "Your granddaughter is the Librarian. I knew she'd be able to help me and find you. And I was right."

Xandie cleared her throat as Lila pushed her gently toward the wounded vampire. "Thanks. But given I was ready to brain you with books, the Library is the one to thank. She knew you were coming and prepared for it."

He winced. "It all worked out in the end."

"But what about the beginning?" Holly's quiet voice filled the room. "What happened to you?"

"That's a story." He cleared his throat. "Hellacious contacted me six months ago. Frantic about something."

"What?" Xandie was more than curious. What would upset someone who raised the dead for a living?

Benoit shrugged and then placed a hand on his chest. "I have no clue. I would not take his call. Whitburn is a two-faced snake."

"Luc," Elspeth growled at her friend.

"Shush, Elspeth. You may have liked the man, but I always saw through his posturing."

Xandie broke in before the two old friends started squabbling. "What does Whitburn contacting you have to do with your wounds?"

"Because since that call, someone's been following me. Then I heard about Hannah and Minerva's death. I decided to come visit Elspeth."

"Safety in numbers?" Lila winked at the vampire.

He smiled briefly. "Something like that. I use a blood donor service. I ring up and they send a volunteer around. Last month, I had a sore fang but couldn't get in to see the dentist. That probably saved my life."

"I swear, you have a morbid fear of medical specialists." Elspeth shook her head, disgusted.

"But it saved my life. The donor turned up, and I fed, but my fang hurt so I stopped feeding. Plus, I was getting a woozy head. Next thing, my donor staked me. I pushed the woman off and stumbled next door for help, but to no avail. So, I immediately left for Point Muse."

"You didn't get help for your wound? Did your donor explain her motive at all?" Holly questioned.

Lila nudged Xandie. "Ooh, look at our Harrow banshee, using detective terms like motive."

"I didn't think the wound was serious and decided discretion was better than valor, and I needed to get to Elspeth as soon as possible. I got a call from my neighbor on the way here. The woman had no memory of attacking me or even coming to my house. She had her regular checkup at the donor service, and the doctor prescribed vitamin C, but otherwise, everything was fine. Next thing, she's at my place, surrounded by PIG agents."

Sounded to Xandie like someone got to the poor woman. But how did the perp know Benoit would call the service right then? "Is the donor service a regular thing?"

Lucien nodded. "I have a regular appointment set up with the company. Same time once a month with the same O positive donor, but she went on holiday a few weeks ago. Some cruise she won. I had to take a relief donor."

Bingo. "Yeah, we've seen that before. Did the doctor say why they prescribed the vitamin C?"

"That's the thing, it wasn't the normal doctor either. The normal one had been called away. A doctor by the name of Burne filled in. I think they prescribed iron, too, but the dose the new donor was given was quadruple the normal amount. That's why I was woozy. Excess iron overwhelms vampiric senses."

Burne. This was becoming a pattern. "The doctor wanted you disoriented so the donor could stake you."

Benoit nodded at Xandie. "I agree. Plus, the PIG agents are fairly sure a memory hex wiped the donor."

"Hexes again," Xandie murmured.

"All my specialties," Elspeth admitted and sagged onto the couch next to her friend. "Most of the hexes you've seen so far have been straight out of the coven's toolbox. I designed them all."

"Kind of a specific thing to do. Use hexes designed by a coven member to kill others in the coven. Someone hates you, Elspeth, really and truly hates you." Xandie stared at her grandmother, brain working overtime. "What about Lucien's amulet piece?" Xandie turned to the wounded vampire. "Do you still have it?"

He smiled wryly. "It goes everywhere with me." Lucien pointed to a decorative tattoo on his upper chest, opposite to his wound.

"Your trickiness will get you dead, Luc."

"Sorry?" Xandie wasn't following.

"Smarty fangs had a scribe transfer the amulet piece into ink and had an Ink Witch tattoo him. He thinks it's foolproof."

"But it is, *ma Coeur*. You must be proud of my deviousness." Lucien smirked at a fuming Elspeth.

"Until the killer cuts out a chunk of your chest and transforms it into the amulet piece."

"Ah, but the killer will be delayed somewhat, and that is if they can even find where my amulet piece hides."

"Who knew about your piece?"

"Only those PIG people." The vampire sneered at the mention of the Paranormal Investigative Group.

Lucien was still a target as much as Elspeth was. They both needed to be under lock and key and watched. *Easier said than done.* "Someone who knows Elspeth, knows her past, is hunting her down with devious tricks."

Elspeth cackled and lights overhead fizzled. "That ain't news."

No, it wasn't. People either hated Elspeth or loved her. No in between for her grandmother.

But stalking victims with her grandmother's own hexes? It was already personal, but now it had taken on a new level of creepy.

ELEVEN

"Don't let that baker cousin of yours catch you munching in here. She might get your grandmother to hex me." Delilah winked as she placed a pot of tea in front of Xandie.

Swallowing her mouthful of fluffy berry pancake, Xandie waved a fork at Delilah. "Elspeth's bark is worse than her bite."

"I doubt that, honey." Delilah cleared off a booth next to Xandie's table.

"I won't tell if you won't." Xandie smiled widely and then forked in another mouthful.

"Tell me you haven't rejected your favorite cousin's baking?" Lila dropped next to Xandie.

"Hey, I thought I was your favorite cousin?" Holly sat opposite Lila and Xandie.

"You have that eau de mortuary perfume going on now. Xandie's musty Library smell is so much better."

"Nothing is sacred in this town, is it?" Xandie fought off a pancake attack from Lila with her fork.

"Nope." Lila successfully stole a generous mouthful of fluffy deliciousness. "Hey, this is good." She waved to Delilah and ordered two more plates of pancakes for her and Holly.

"Did you hunt me down at the diner because we have another Elspeth incident or a dead body?"

Holly shook her head. "Nope to both of those things, and I haven't had another vision either."

"We just wanted to see if you had anything new from the Library."

"Actually, Lila, the Library's given me an *information pending* message. Jackson letting me look at those two files helped the Library get me access. It's just a matter of waiting and hoping no one dies in the meantime."

"Where are the files then?" Lila snuck another pancake morsel and chewed her mouthful victoriously.

Xandie scowled at Lila and hunched protectively over her plate. "I left them in the kitchen at home.

Theo is supposedly guarding them. I think he's trying to gather dirt on Elspeth."

Delilah cleared her throat and deposited pancakes and syrup in front of Lila and Holly. "Here you go, Harrows. Did I hear you mention bodies? Surely we don't have any more." Delilah shuddered. "I thought I left all that behind when I moved to Point Muse."

Holly nodded sagely. "Pretty much everyone assumes that when they move here. In reality, our accidental death statistics are higher than the city of Portland."

Delilah shuddered and then wandered back off to the kitchen, muttering under her breath.

"So speaks Death Girl," Lila intoned with a serious look on her face before collapsing into her seat with the giggles.

"Mom told you not to call me that," Holly growled at Lila and lifted her fork in a stabbing motion.

Xandie put her hands up in a time out. "Can we focus on dead bodies and killers, please?"

"What's there to focus on? Someone's killing Morrigan Coven members for their fragments of the super scary Morpheus Amulet. And Elspeth is in the thick of it. At least this time, we're fairly sure she isn't the perpetrator."

"This time?" Xandie choked on her last mouthful of pancake. "There's been other times when Elspeth's been accused of murder?" A bit much even from a mayhem-inclined Harrow witch.

Lila waved Xandie's question away. "Occasionally Braun or the Feds come calling about someone they've dug up or who has gone missing. But Elspeth always wiggles out of anything official. The old girl has serious evasion skills."

Every family had a black sheep—the Harrows just had a hag instead. "We're agreed that Elspeth and her bit of the amulet is a target? Do we have any other information to go on?"

"Oh." Holly raised a hand. "Well, it's not information, but I got through to Aunt Amelia and Mom last night. I gave them a heavily edited version of what's going on. They're going to speak to someone on the cruise. See what information they can dig up."

Xandie nodded. "That's a start. A person by the name of Burne left the tickets for the delivery driver from the grocery store. Braun updated me this morning. The grocery guy remembered the name." *Burne?* Something niggled at the back of Xandie's mind. She'd heard that last name somewhere else before.

"Do we get the old girls and Colin back from the cruise?" Lila grimaced. "Interrupt their floating singles' bar on the slight chance someone offs Elspeth? Do we risk it?"

"It doesn't matter. As of today, they're between ports for the next forty-eight hours before we can contact them again."

"Right. We deal with this ourselves. I have the files at home and the Library will get us access soon. Hopefully, we'll be able to pinpoint the suspects, maybe even work out our next move."

Lila look confused for a moment at Xandie's words. "*Suspects?* I thought we pretty much worked out that necromancer, Whitburn, was our culprit?"

"I want to be sure. This is our grandmother. I need to be positive. The Library will give me access to the information soon. That will help us be one hundred percent certain."

"If it raises dead pets like a necromancer and plays with dead people like a necromancer, it *is* a necromancer." Lila stood and dropped money on the table. "I say we focus on the lover of dead things. He smells stinky to me."

Holly pushed away from the table and stomped to the door. "I swear, any more cracks about dead things and smells and I'll steal one of Elspeth's hexes. Watch out then, baker girl."

Lila rolled her eyes. "What a way to insult me. I *am* a baker girl. Seriously, you're a Harrow. Where is your originality?"

"Stick your Harrow originality up your sugary iced buns." Holly shoved the door of the diner open and waited for her cousins to join her.

Honestly, anyone unfamiliar with the cousins would think they hated each other. But beneath the squabbling was the easy familiarity of family and the knowledge that no matter what, they'd always be there for each other. *Even when you don't want them to be.*

Xandie joined her sniping cousins just as Deputy Melody Braun scooted to a halt in front of them.

"Oh-oh. Who's on Elspeth duty?" Xandie winced, sure she knew what was coming.

"Lila told me Buchanan was. Or was that more of this Harrow originality you spoke of?" Holly glared at an innocent looking Lila.

"Hey, hey. No blame games. Buchanan told me he had Elspeth watch this morning. He wanted to try to squeeze more Morrigan information out of her." She spread her hands open. "Can't blame me if he took his eye off the hag."

Melody bent over and nested her hands on her knees as she panted. "I swear, no more honey buns." Letting out a deep breath, she straightened. "Your grandmother escaped Buchanan. Apparently, she is about to hex Rose Mayweather at the Inn."

Xandie gritted her teeth. "Why is Elspeth at the Inn?"

"Seems Rose offered a free room to someone named Bridget if she did a psychic reading for the other guests. Elspeth found out. Best get there ASAP."

Melody straightened her uniform and then made a detour directly to Lila's bakery.

"If Melody's overdosing on Lila's honey buns, then the situation is bad." Xandie pointed to Holly's hot-pink moped. "You're up, speed demon."

Holly rubbed her hands and intoned in a pseudo-dramatic voice, "Buckle up, buttercup. You are in for a wild ride."

"Better you than me, Librarian. I'll pray to Hecate you get there in one piece." With a waggle of her fingers, Lila strode off to her bakery.

Xandie clambered on behind her cousin and clinched her helmet on tight. For the quietest and least dramatic of the three cousins, Holly drove like a maniac. But then again, when Elspeth had her hex on, no one was safe.

Speed, it was.

"How would you like a bun with that bouffant hairdo?" Elspeth stood on a chair, a hard dinner roll in hand.

Bridget shrieked and covered her crystal ball. "You haven't changed at all, you vindictive hag."

Xandie closed her eyes for a moment. Try as she might, she couldn't blot out the sight of her grandmother perched on a chair and the ex-Morrigan Coven member, Bridget, surrounded by a pile of hard rolls.

"You fix this, Meyers. You hear me?" Rose Mayweather, owner of the Mayweather Inn, poked Xandie in the ribs as the innkeeper cowered behind her.

She needed a pay rise. "Hey, Elspeth. I think you dropped something?" Xandie held up her grandmother's hip flask and shook it, making sure the sloshing noise of liquid moving carried to Elspeth's elderly ears.

Like a predator sensing blood, Elspeth jerked her head toward Xandie and the flask.

"This is why you're my favorite." Elspeth climbed down from the chair and threw her last roll over her shoulder at Bridget.

Xandie ignored the high-pitched squeal from Bridget as the roll hit her forehead. She drew Elspeth in with the promise of a swig of Witchshine.

In a choreographed move, Holly swept in and moved Elspeth to the back corner of the dining room, away from bread missiles.

"She was a menace back then, and she's a menace now." Bridget straightened and dusted off her crystal ball.

"At least I'm not a sell-out," Elspeth hollered.

"I have a gift that helps others. That's not selling out."

"It is if you get paid for it. There's a word for that."

"*Elspeth*," the horrified Xandie protested.

Elspeth nodded. "That's right. Fortune-teller. That's what you are."

Xandie sagged in relief. For a moment, she thought Elspeth had meant...

"Drugs, woman? You drugged me?" Buchanan roared from the entryway.

"Oops." Elspeth dropped out of sight behind Holly.

Bridget pointed a red-tipped nail straight at Elspeth. "She's hiding in the corner. She called me a fortune-teller. Throw the book at her."

Elspeth peered around Holly at Buchanan. "You're old. It's not my fault you fell asleep."

"Fell asleep?" Buchanan growled. "I drank that horrendous mix you call a smoothie, and I passed out with my head on your table. You drugged me."

Holly rolled her eyes and whispered to Xandie, "You take any kind of beverage off Elspeth and you're asking to be drugged. No one is that stupid in Point Muse anymore."

Elspeth sniffed. "Not my fault you can't hold your smoothie."

"This is why you can't trust her. She's crazy." Bridget grabbed a tablecloth off a neighboring table and polished her crystal ball.

Elspeth shoved past Holly and shook the hand that held her flask at Bridget. "I was never crazy, and *I* wasn't the one who crossed a line. That was you and the rest of the coven."

Bridget drew herself up, outrage in every curve of her plump body. "We did our duty. We weren't responsible for the one rotten egg in the carton. You, with all your plots and conspiracy theories, caused the drama. You live on secrets."

Elspeth's eyes grew wide, and her top lip drew back from her teeth as she opened her mouth.

"Yes, Mother, why don't you spill some of your secrets and tell us all exactly what's going on and who's after your wrinkled hide this time?" Amelia Harrow, middle daughter and Lila's mother, stood with hands on her skinny hips and a scowl on her tanned face.

Winifred, Elspeth's youngest daughter and Holly's mother, peeked out from behind her elder sister's back and giggled when a junior Paladin agent standing with Buchanan winked in her direction.

"What are they doing back? They were on that singles' cruise. Supposedly out of our hair?" Xandie hissed at Holly.

"The last I heard they were out of contact for forty-eight hours. I have no clue how they got back or who told them Elspeth was in trouble."

"My bones told me. They always ache when Elspeth is up to mayhem." Amelia fixed an accusing eye on her mother. "An ex-coven member trying to kill you? Really, Mother? Only you could make someone hate you enough to kill."

"No one is gonna hurt my dame." Colin strutted

out from between Amelia's legs, red-colored zinc cream spread across his nose.

"Love your skin protection, Colin." Xandie bit a smile back at the mouthy pug. Elspeth had played Doctor Frankenstein with the pug in the hopes of making him gold medal worthy material in the Supernatural Pet and Familiar Show. He'd won due to the fact most of the competitors had been killed off —*literally*—by a murderous monster. Now the cigar-smoking, food-inhaling, humping-obsessed pug had become part of the family.

"Gotta protect this manly bod." Colin puffed out his chest and twerked his hips in a manic circle.

Holly slapped a hand over her eyes. "Let me know when he's done. My brain can't handle the image of a pug gyrating."

"Mother?" Like a dog with a bone, Amelia kept her focus on Elspeth.

"What? I can't help it if you couldn't even let loose on a singles' cruise." Elspeth shrugged. "Not my fault they kicked you off. You need one of my potions."

"Do. Not. Distract. Me."

Winifred raised a hand like a naughty schoolgirl. "Actually, they tried to talk her into staying. She's the new limbo champ. She swept the betting pool."

Chortling, Elspeth waved a bread roll overhead and cheered. "Well, that sounds like a little of my DNA finally showing up. You have no idea how loose I was when I was a young woman."

"Stop."

"Mother."

"Elspeth."

Everyone's cringing protests collided as Buchanan roared, "Enough." Waiting for silence, he nodded as everyone shut up. "Ladies, you were on a cruise arranged by our suspect. Did you happen to see anything of note?"

Amelia grimaced. "We questioned the cruise director, but all she knew was the name of the person who'd organized the tickets. Apparently, quite a few were bought in bulk. We weren't the only ones there who'd supposedly won tickets."

"Let me guess. Alberta Burne?" That alias kept showing up. Xandie

rubbed her forehead with a weapon-free hand. There was a connection, a link she was missing. The Library would be disappointed with her sleuthing, but when your family was on the line, the stakes became raised, and the level of pressure escalated, causing a brain-fog to drift in.

"Exactly right. Paid with a credit card in the

name of Hellacious Whitburn. But I'm gathering that's not a surprise." Agent Jackson dipped a sweeping bow in Elspeth's daughters' direction and caused Winifred to titter again. "Ladies, may I ask how you knew to come home?"

Winifred fluttered her eyes at the agent. "My daughter's phone call was suspiciously absent of detail, and she kept trying to distract us by asking questions about the cruise." She shook her wild reddish-brown curls. "What grown-up daughter wants details about her mother's singles' cruise? The jig was up then. We blackmailed the cruise with a fake limbo-related injury, and the company flew us back in on an enchanted carpet this morning."

Amelia growled. "We also found out Colin gets magic carpet sick. Not the most pleasant few hours I've spent." She rounded on the pug that had sidled over to Elspeth's old coven member. "I told you you'd regret that last prawn cocktail."

"Ya gotta live in the moment or regret the past, doll face." Colin nudged Bridget. "How you doin'?"

Bridget cast a perplexed glance down at the pug. "This animal has something on his nose."

That was the weirdest thing that struck the woman about a talking dog? "Uh, Ms. Doyle?" Xandie tried to get the older woman's attention.

Transferring her attention away from Colin, Bridget shook a fist at Elspeth. "Don't try and distract me. Someone needs to take that menace of a witch in hand."

Colin twined his body around Bridget's legs. "Oh, no one controls my Elspeth. She's an original."

Clearing her throat, Xandie tried again. "Ms. Doyle? You really need to move…"

"I will not move from this spot unless that woman leaves first." She pointed to a snickering Elspeth. "Stop laughing at me, Harrow."

"I will when you watch out for perving pugs." Elspeth bent over, her cackles echoing through the dining room.

Bridget squealed when she realized that Colin had positioned himself so he could stare up her gauzy, floaty skirt. "You disgusting animal. Back, filthy dog."

Colin shook his head like a bumble bee had stung him in his neck rolls. "I should have known better than to hang out under the skirts of Elspeth's nemesis. She's one of *those* women."

"I know I'll regret asking, but what kind of woman?" Holly bit her lip, looking equal parts curious and worried.

"*Cat lover.* She has hot-pink cats on her drawers." Colin shuddered. "I'll need a whole-body cleanse just to deal with the trauma."

"You." Bridget glared at Elspeth. "This is all you. I can see your meddling claws in that abomination's face."

Elspeth drew herself up. "Abomination? How dare you insult my beautiful boy?" She held up her fists. "Bring it, fortune-teller."

Screeching, Bridget rushed forward, hands slapping the air in front of her.

Xandie hip-checked Bridget off course and grabbed a bread roll off the table and threw it to Holly, who deftly caught it and shoved it into Elspeth's open mouth.

Buchanan stepped in and hoisted Elspeth over a shoulder and carried her out, dislodging the bread roll in the process.

Elspeth's holler was muffled as she bumped against Buchanan's back. "I swear you'll regret coming here, fortune-teller. Got me? R. E. G. R. E. T." Elspeth spelled out the last word.

Everyone sagged in relief as the Paladin and upside-down witch disappeared from sight.

"I wonder if it's time to consider Eternal Springs Retirement Home. I think she's getting worse." Amelia wrinkled her nose. "And Colin, you know

I'm an animal empath and can read you? You set that entire scene up."

Colin wiggled his tail in an energetic circle. "One way to get Elspeth out of the room. Besides, I really saw cats. I took one for the team."

Winifred shot forward and corralled Colin under an arm. "Yes, dearest boy. We're lucky to have you. Now don't upset Amelia. You know she's the town veterinarian. I'd hate it if you ended up in her clinic for a nasty snip-snip surgery."

"And people say I'm obsessed. That's all you dames talk about." Colin sniffed as Winifred followed a stomping Amelia out of the dining room.

"I swear, I'm this close to banning all Harrows from the Inn." Rose held up her hand and measured two fingers apart.

"The last Harrow to set foot in the Inn was Xandie when you had that plague of rats."

Rose gasped. "Holly Harrow, how dare you suggest the Inn was in any way liable for that rodent invasion? It was caused by a psychotic dragon."

Xandie held her hands up. "And I'm a Meyers, remember?"

"Close enough." Rose shook her head and a large curl of silvery blonde hair fell across her forehead from her beehive bouffant. "I will ban you all, Harrows and extended Harrows."

"If we suffer, you have to suffer, too, cousin. That's the Harrow code." Holly kicked a bread roll out of the way and headed outside.

Rose pointed a trembling finger at the pyramid of rolls near Bridget's feet. "I expect that mess to be cleaned, Librarian. Do you understand?"

Without waiting for acknowledgement, the inn owner stomped off.

With a sigh, Xandie bent down, collected all the rolls, and dumped them on the table.

"I don't know how you put up with her. She's pure mayhem." Bridget sidled over to Xandie and pasted a commiserating smile upon her face.

"From what I can tell, Elspeth stopped a black marketer and possibly saved thousands of lives. Doesn't sound like mayhem to me."

"It's all in the delivery." Bridget lovingly lifted the crystal ball from the table and cradled it like a baby.

"If you hate Elspeth so much, why come to Point Muse?"

"No matter how I feel about her, we're Morrigan. She might drive me crazy, but you protect your own." Bridget nodded to Xandie and strolled out.

"Bridget? Do you have a piece of the Morpheus Amulet?"

Bridget stalled for a moment but didn't turn. "You think that's why the others were killed? For their amulet pieces?"

"Don't you?"

The Morrigan member continued her walk. "I hope not. For my sake." With that, she disappeared.

"That answered that question." Elspeth's nemesis definitely had a piece of the amulet.

Which meant Bridget, along with Elspeth and Lucien, were at the top of a very short hit list.

TWELVE

"Kill me now." Xandie winced as the siren screamed over her head. She thought that after getting Elspeth out of Mayweather Inn, she'd have a chance to relax. A hot chocolate or a hot tea, late-night B-grade movie, and a good snooze on the couch.

"What? Did you say tuna?" Theo yelled back at Xandie. Horatio, Theo's pet imp, ears stuffed full of cotton wool, cowered on Theo's back.

"I said..." Xandie yelled and then gave up. She'd arrived back from Elspeth duty to Theo and Horatio locked out of the house and the current state of noise pollution.

Agent Jackson slid to a stop just in front of Chief Braun, both breathing quickly as they tried to talk over the other.

"Take this…"

"These are spelled…"

Xandie glared at the men, both holding earmuffs out to her. "Seriously? You couldn't have come up with this an hour ago?"

"Earmuffs," Theo squealed and clawed Braun's leg until he dropped his pair to the ground. Shaking Horatio off, Theo wiggled on the ground and slid the earmuffs over his ears. He sighed in relief and sagged back onto the grass.

"Either my head is ridiculously small, or Theo's deformed." Xandie shrugged and swiped Jackson's earmuffs, sliding them on. Instant relief hit her as the noisy siren cut out completely.

"They've been spelled, so they mute the siren, but you can still hear what's going on around you."

Xandie smiled a little. She still hadn't forgiven him for attempting to wipe her memory, but noise blocking earmuffs was a start. "Can you tell me what the heck is going on? Why are we locked out of the house and the Library in the middle of the night?"

"What? What did you say?" Braun raised his voice over the siren.

Agent Jackson hadn't seen fit to share spelled ear protection with the Point Muse Police Chief.

Xandie pointed to her spotlighted driveway and the gaggle of pajama-clad onlookers now gawking at them.

With a nod, Braun strode off to move the nosy gossips along.

"Any reason you didn't issue our Chief spelled headgear?"

Agent Jackson smirked. "He didn't ask nicely enough."

Xandie rolled her eyes but refused to comment. She had other more important issues to focus on. "Why has the Library locked us out, and why has her alarm triggered?"

Theo stopped his lolling on the ground and straightened. "I can answer that. Some woman with red hair delivered a parcel. I took it into the Library. The next thing I know, Horatio and I were shoved outside, and the alarm goes off. That's when you turned up."

"I worked that out with all your yowling. But why did the Library shut down?"

"Elspeth has an idea on that." Lila stepped up next to Xandie and gave Theo a rub underneath his chin.

"Oh, please, enlighten us on Ms. Harrow's working theory," Agent Jackson replied with eyebrows arched, his tone heavily laced with sarcasm.

Xandie coughed to hide the laughter bubbling up. The oh-so-competent agent didn't enjoy relinquishing control to someone else... especially not the slightly haggish Elspeth Harrow.

"Raise both those eyebrows at Elspeth and she'll have those caterpillars off your face in a flash." Lila grinned, teeth on show.

Jackson cleared his throat and inclined his head. "Be happy to hear any theory Ms. Harrow has."

"From Theo's description of the parcel, Elspeth could identify the surname of the sender."

"And?" Braun finally joined them.

"The surname was Burne. That's the alias Whitburn used to use. She didn't recognize the first name. Alberta. But Whitburn always liked to disguise himself as a female during certain Morrigan Coven operations."

Lila delivered the words with a satisfied expression.

Xandie studied her cousin's face. She was just that little too pleased with herself. "What did you do?"

"*Moi*? I've done nothing."

"So, why look so pleased with yourself?"

Lila sniffed, affront in every line of her body. "The lack of faith from my cousin offends me."

"And?"

"And I bribed Elspeth with moonshine and mom's chocolate stash and told Elspeth Holly broke her favorite cauldron when we were little. Elspeth gave up the information and is happily cursing Holly now." Lila beamed. "All is good in Lila Harrow's world."

Shaking her head, Xandie turned to Braun and Jackson. "How long until we can get inside the Library? There are files in there we need."

Jackson turned to Braun. "You know Library protocol and security better than I. What's your best guess?"

"Anywhere from a few hours to a few days, maybe more, depending on the level of threat to the Library. Obviously, the parcel was contaminated or contained some kind of threat, physical or magical, to the Library." Braun shrugged. "The Library will clear the threat, but until then, you and Theo are homeless."

"Great." The Library was her home. Now she couldn't even open the front door.

Jackson winked at Xandie. "My room at the Inn has two beds in it. Happy to offer the spare to our very important Librarian and her feline companion."

"Braun Lodge has plenty of rooms. Aggie thinks of Xandie like family." Braun glowered at the PIG agent and moved to stand close to Xandie.

Moving to stand on the other side of Xandie, Jackson faced Braun down. "From what I can gather, you and Xandie have a contentious relationship, and Braun Lodge isn't exactly quiet with all your bear shifter siblings in and out. The Inn and my room are quiet enough she can get some rest."

"From what I hear, you wiped her memories and made her come to Point Muse. Why would she want to stay with you?" Braun pointed a finger tipped with a claw at the PIG agent.

Jackson whipped out a metal wand and tapped Braun's bear claw. "Unless you want to lose any memories you have of how to shift into a bear, I'd retract that claw."

Xandie stepped away from the testosterone-smothered space between the two men. "You know what? Being homeless seems more appealing now." Both men ignored Xandie.

Lila nudged her cousin. "You know Harrow House is open to all Harrows and Library felines."

Great. Stuck in Harrow House with her talking

cat, his pet imp, her cousin, her hex-mad grand-mother, a fanged freeloader, and their Paladin jailer. "Yay," Xandie offered weakly. At least it was better than a hotel room with Jackson or Braun Lodge with Zach and his siblings.

Lila waved at the still squabbling law enforce-ment officers and steered Xandie toward her lumi-nescent blue bakery van. "Just to show I care, I'm moving in, too. Added protection. It'll be a party."

"Or a wake..."

"Feed me. Feed me." Theo punctuated each word with a swipe of his paw across Xandie's nose.

Xandie squinted through one eye at her food obsessed feline. "Didn't I just feed you?"

"That was last night when we arrived in this witch's den of hexing. You've slept most of the day away. Feed me. Feed me." This time, Theo unsheathed his claws and rested them threateningly against the tender skin of Xandie's nose tip.

"Stop torturing me, you sadistic animal." Xandie rolled over and pushed herself out of bed with a groan. At least she, Theo, and Horatio had a place to sleep, but it wasn't a patch on her Library home.

Xandie stood and stretched the kinks out of her back.

"Food," Theo wailed. Horatio punctuated his owner's cry with shrill pips and a raised fist.

Anyone would think she starved them. But, judging by the cat's potbelly, he was doing fine. Xandie held a hand up. "Let's head to the kitchen, and we'll agree you never touch my nose again." Xandie opened the door and shuffled downstairs, passing Elspeth whispering on the phone.

"Wow, the dead walk." Lila munched on an apple as Xandie entered the kitchen diner.

Holly threw a cookie at Lila. "Hey, enough with the dead jokes. It's a sensitive subject, especially at the moment."

"It was a joke, banshee. You need to lighten up."

"I'll show you a joke." Holly launched herself at Lila, only to be caught by Buchanan, who dropped her back into a chair.

He continued on toward the coffee pot and poured himself a cup as though that didn't just happen. "Do you Harrows ever not fight?"

Xandie snorted and opened the fridge, grabbing out a fresh plate of tuna. She knelt and placed it on the floor for Theo and Horatio. "Is the sky blue today?"

"Are we Harrows?" Lila smirked and threw an apple core at Holly.

"Are we breathing?" Holly caught the core and then lobbed it at Xandie.

Xandie ducked, and the core hit Elspeth in the chest before dropping to the floor.

All eyes swiveled to Elspeth, who picked the core up and carefully placed it on the bench. She ran a hand over the top of the apple and watched with an enormous smile is it shriveled down to a dry husk. She looked up, maintaining the smile. "Have you ever heard the story of the witch who littered?"

All the girls and Buchanan shook their heads.

Elspeth cackled, and the coffee pot overflowed with volcanic ferocity. "Really? I thought such a tragic story would be required learning for young witches keen on survival."

Amelia stepped into the kitchen, with Winifred in tow. "Are you still telling that old tale to scare young witches? You trotted it out whenever we didn't pick up after ourselves."

Winifred shuddered. "It used to give me nightmares imagining what happened to that poor, young witch."

"Get a grip, Winnie. The old girl was just scaring you into cleaning for her." Colin trotted in. "Look at all my dames in the one spot. Warms an old pug to his cockles."

"The less we know about your cockles, the better, dog." Lila took a step away from Colin as he raised a back leg next to her.

Theo hissed at the pug. "No manners at all. Doginstein."

Colin dropped his leg and casually sat back. "You do know that no one other than the Librarian can hear your insults, feline?"

"I'm sure Elspeth can help with that minor issue. She made you talk, didn't she? After all, I am family." Theo smirked and twitched his tail in Colin's face.

"Claiming family rights? I see tuna breath has settled in." Colin turned to Xandie. "Are you sure he didn't break the Library just to get pampered at Harrow House?"

"Pampered, my furry tush. The service in this house is abysmal, as is your company." Theo tipped his nose in the air and pranced past Colin, just as a low rumbling shook the dining room and a putrid fishy smell filled the air.

Xandie slapped a hand over her face as the stench wafted over. Next to her, both Lila and Holly doubled over, gagging.

Colin shook his head at Theo. "And you talk about manners, feline."

Arching his back, Theo yowled, fur standing upright. "I would never desecrate Harrow House like that. Don't pass the blame like you passed the wind, you miscreant."

"Oooh. Big words for a stinky tuna lover no one else can hear," Colin sneered back.

"Enough." Elspeth slammed her hands together, and a large boom sounded. A cool wind blew through the house, blowing the tuna-scented flatulence out of the kitchen.

Amelia, with eyes watering, took a deep breath. "I told you Colin can't have tuna. It disagrees with his constitution. You need to be a responsible pet owner."

"Colin is his own man." Elspeth waved her hand in the air. "Pug, that is."

Buchanan massaged his forehead, unmoved by the putrid stench bomb that had just erupted in the kitchen. "Maybe we could focus on the coven killer and protecting Elspeth?"

"Speaking of that..." Elspeth turned to Buchanan. "What's with all the shifter guards arriving? I'm sure one hexed dead shifter is enough, don't you think?"

With an oath, Buchanan stormed out, muttering, "Damn local cops pushing their noses into Paladin business."

With a malevolent smile, Elspeth disappeared out to her workshop.

"Since when has Elspeth been helpful to law enforcement?" Theo paused in his offended stalk out of the room.

Xandie straightened. "While I've been living in Point Muse, Elspeth has never helped aid law and order."

Holly joined her cousin. "Not in my entire lifetime."

Winifred closed her eyes for a moment. "Mother has a pathological distrust of rules and regulations. She'd never willingly volunteer anything to help an officer of the law."

"She's scarpered." Amelia sat down at the kitchen table. "Her regular modus operandi. Distract and disappear."

Xandie cleared her throat. "Elspeth was on the phone when I came past this morning. I couldn't hear what she was saying though."

Lila licked her lips. "I think we have an Elspeth alert. Holly, check the phone. Xandie, see what's going on outside. I'll search Elspeth's workshop.

Now break." Lila clapped her hands, and all three girls shot off in different directions. Their aunts watched them go with resigned expressions on their faces.

Xandie raced to the front door, and Harrow House obligingly swung open. She patted the door frame as she passed through. Even Harrow House was looking out for the irascible Elspeth.

"What's the rush?" Braun leaned against the porch, enjoying the sight of a flustered Xandie.

Halting her run to the outside, Xandie patted her bed-hair down. Thanks to her long nap, her shoulder-length brown hair was sticking up and out like tufts of fur. At least she wasn't in pajamas, thanks to Lila. She was in a comfy pair of yoga pants and *A Harrow Witch Does It Better* T-shirt. She pasted on a smile. "Nothing's wrong. Just checking on the situation outside."

"Situation?" Braun parroted Xandie's words, but with a mocking twist.

Damn man. "Elspeth was concerned about using shifter guards since her crow friend already died from a hex that target shifters. That's all." *And if you believe that, maybe I can sell you a hypothetical bridge.*

Xandie glanced around the yard. Buchanan was

arguing with Aggie Braun with a pile of shifters grouped around them. The Paladins had formed a wider circle around the group and still had guards posted. Surely Elspeth couldn't escape with all the manpower around Harrow House?

"Checking to see if any blood's been shed yet, or checking on something else?" Braun straightened and sniffed the air. "Or should I say someone else?"

Xandie raised a hand and backed inside the house. "I have no clue what you're babbling about."

Harrow House slammed the door in Braun's face.

"Thanks for the save, House." Xandie spun around as Holly slapped the phone down.

"We have a problem, Xandie."

"Yep, a big one." Lila came out from the kitchen and agreed with Holly. "Elspeth isn't in the workshop or in the house."

"I snuck into her bedroom, and the old girl is definitely missing in action. But I found this sweet hat." Colin wiggled his hips while wearing an Elspeth-special cone brassiere on his head.

Shuddering at the horrifying image of a bra-decorated pug twerking, Xandie whipped the bra off Colin's head and tucked it under her arm. "She could be anywhere. Where do we start looking?"

"Buzzkill," Colin muttered. "I'm off. There has to be someone wearing a dress around here." He wandered off to find a stray skirt to peer up.

"I think I can help with finding a place to look." Holly pointed to the phone. "I checked who the last caller was."

"And?"

"Mayweather Inn was the last number."

Xandie groaned. The current abode of Bridget Doyle, ex-Morrigan Coven member and Elspeth's fortune-telling nemesis. "Right, Elspeth probably ducked out for a second round of bread rolls with Bridget."

Lila dangled her bakery van keys in front of her cousins. "Well, post haste, little Librarian and wailing banshee. We've got a hex-mad grandmother to catch before she incites the rage of Aphrodite wannabe, Rose Mayweather."

Xandie flung the front door open and moved to step out. Unfortunately, the broad chest of muscled bear shifter, Zach Braun, provided a barricade to their get-Elspeth plans.

"Now where would you meddling Harrow women be off to?" He crossed his arms over his chest and smirked.

The cousins shared a look. Xandie sighed. It was

her turn to provide a distraction. "Lila had something urgent come up, and Holly and I are going along for moral support." Ducking her head, she smiled coquettishly up at the brawny police chief.

Lila and Holly sidled past Braun and power-walked to Lila's van and leaned against it, watching Xandie.

"Urgent? Nothing to do with Elspeth ducking out?" He dropped his hands and rested against the open door.

His large shoulders filled the doorway and Xandie felt a wave of heat rise from her throat. Zach Braun had been a thorn in her side whenever she investigated a murder. But lately he'd been easygoing and willing to work with her...*mostly*. Now Xandie was noticing how his shaggy hair flopped over his forehead, and her hands itched to push it back out of the way. She wiped her hands on her yoga pants, forgetting Elspeth's bra under her arm. The brassiere slipped and landed on the floor between them.

They both stared at the underwear, laying cone-up on the ground.

"Was the urgent task related to updating underwear?"

Where's a stray hole I could fall into when I needed it? "It's Elspeth's. Colin was dancing around with it on his head. I just forgot I was holding onto it." Xandie reached down at the same time Braun did to pick up the bra, and their heads collided with a meaty thump.

Braun grabbed Xandie's shoulders and steadied her as she wobbled back.

"You okay there, Xandie?"

Xandie, not the typical sarcastic Meyers. A shiver ziplined down Xandie's spine. His ice-blue eyes bored into her amber Harrow ones. She cleared her throat, breaking the physical spell he'd entrapped her in. "I'm fine, Zach. Sorry about that." She smiled weakly and rubbed the slight lump on her head.

Zach helped Xandie stand, still holding onto one hand. "I'm used to contrary Harrows and Meyers."

"That's us. Contrary." How on earth did she get herself in this position? It was supposed to be about distracting the shifter from questioning their exit, not counting the number of times his biceps flexed.

"Are you going to tell me the actual reason you three are skipping out on Harrow House and your protection?"

"Lila has some female business. We're giving her sister solidarity." *When in doubt, embarrass.*

Zach tilted his head back and guffawed, the tanned line of his throat bare to view. Tiny elephants stomped through the pit of her stomach as she asked, "You don't believe me?"

"Your middle name is sneaky, and I have a sister and a meddling mother who both used the same excuse when they wanted to ditch us." He sobered a little. "How about I conveniently forget I saw you, but if you have any trouble with your complicated shenanigans, call me first?"

"And if I don't?"

"You'll owe me a coffee date at Lila's."

Had Braun just asked her out on a date?

"Why don't we just skip to a coffee date after this Elspeth fiasco is over? Since we both know you'll end up in trouble, anyway." He winked at Xandie.

"If you're done flirting, we gotta be someplace." Lila grabbed Xandie's arm and tugged her away. "She says yes. Call her to set up a time. Ciao, shifter."

"Why did you do that?" hissed Xandie.

"Because you two are painfully slow, and with that PIG agent sniffing around you, Braun needs some encouragement."

"Xandie?" Braun raised his voice, so it traveled to the fleeing women.

Yanking her arm out of Lila's grip, she turned

around just in time to be hit in the face by a flying brassiere.

"You forgot your underwear." He snickered and waved goodbye.

"Elspeth's underwear. Not mine. Elspeth's," Xandie hollered at the back-to-annoying police chief.

"Nice to know that some things never change." Lila giggled and shoved Xandie into her van next to Holly.

This is all my grandmother's fault. Babysitting Elspeth Harrow should come with danger pay.

THIRTEEN

"I'm telling you, Elspeth isn't here." Rose Mayweather, Inn proprietor, shifted in Xandie's direction. "Just because you can't keep track of one old woman doesn't mean that she's hiding here."

"She spoke to someone from the Inn a little while ago. Maybe about an hour?" Who knows what her grandmother was planning? The woman skewed toward dramatic, over-the-top schemes. Xandie shuddered. They needed to find her and lock her in Harrow House and throw away the key.

"She could give a sugar overdosed toddler a run for her money," Lila mumbled under her breath. "Tell me again why Holly got to stay behind in the van and keep a lookout for Elspeth?"

"Because you lost rock, paper, scissors. Stop

being a sore loser," Xandie whispered back, then focused on Rose Mayweather. "Think of all the expensive damage Elspeth could do while hiding out here." Xandie appealed to the innkeeper's business senses. "You know how tricky our grandmother is. For an old girl, she's fast and devious. Is there a possibility she could have snuck in while your back was turned?"

Rose opened her mouth and then closed it again before speaking. "I got a call there was an issue with the kitchen staff, but when I investigated, they denied any problem."

"How long were you gone for?" Lila tapped the front desk with a blunt-tipped nail.

"Only ten minutes. I swear."

Xandie and Lila exchanged a communicative glance.

"Probably enough time for Elspeth to slip upstairs to Bridget Doyle's room."

Rose slumped against the reception desk. "There's no getting rid of you Harrows, is there?"

Lila beamed. "Nope. Best to nip the Harrow in the bud so to speak. Minimizes the damage later."

Giving in, the inn owner slammed a key down on the desk. "Bridget Doyle's room. Any damage you find, you pay for. I'm not sure she's even there, though. She canceled her lunch order to her room this morning. I assumed she was heading out."

With a nod of thanks, Xandie pocketed the key and followed Lila's fast retreating back as her cousin power-walked the stairs to Bridget's room. Xandie blew out a shuddering breath as she pulled up next to Lila.

"Maybe I should start offering healthier options at the bakery? Besides, now you've got Braun asking you on dates, you'll want to keep your girly figure."

"Can we keep our mind on business, please? Besides, I haven't worked out yet how I got roped into a coffee date with the police chief."

"That would be the bubbling tension between the two of you. Had to come to a head sometime."

Cousins. Xandie pointed to the already slightly ajar door. "Can we focus on the open door instead of my lack of fitness and potentially awkward date with the bear shifter?" Reaching out, she pushed the door wide.

"No dead body. No dead body," Lila chanted behind her.

No corpse, but one heck of a mess. Xandie pushed the upside-down bedside table out of the way. The mattress had been shoved off the bed frame and sliced open, springs poking through jagged tears.

Sheets and blankets were shredded into strips which now decorated the floor. The wardrobe doors hung open, the clothing dumped in a corner and shredded.

"Rose's housekeeping skills are worse than Holly's." Lila wrinkled her nose as she peered around.

"No sign of Elspeth or Bridget? Whatever happened, we're too late." But had tornado Elspeth destroyed the room or was it the killer? No amulet was visible either.

"Was this mess caused by an old-woman-on-woman catfight or by the killer searching for Doyle's portion of the amulet?"

Xandie was saved from answering Lila's question by the ear-piercing scream of Rose Mayweather.

"What has your grandmother done to my lovely room?" Rose shoved Xandie out of the way and turned in a full circle on the spot, taking in the destruction. "I hope Elspeth has money squirreled away because she's paying for every single damaged item in this room." Rose stopped spinning and glared at Xandie and Lila, hands on hips.

Lila mirrored the irate woman's body language and glared back. "The door was open. Anyone could have wandered in and trashed the place. Has anyone even seen Elspeth here?"

"What about Bridget? It's her room—did anyone see her leave? Or hear anything?" Xandie peeped out into the corridor. Bridget's room was one of the last at the end of the row, but she had a neighbor on each side. If those rooms were occupied, surely the occupants would have heard something?

Rose lowered her hands and cleared her throat. "About that. One of the rooms next to her is empty, but the other just checked out a few minutes ago. They mentioned they heard glass breaking. They poked their head out into the corridor and spotted a tall, athletic woman exiting the room."

"That leaves out both Bridget *and* Elspeth. No one could accuse them of being athletic. It lets Elspeth off the hook for the room damages. Doesn't it, Rose?" Xandie arched an eyebrow.

"I suppose. Who pays for this mess then?" Rose flapped her hands at the surrounding chaos.

"I'd say the Paranormal Investigative Group has deep pockets, don't they? They're supposed to be keeping an eye on Elspeth and her friends, so bill them."

Rose beamed at Lila and blew her a kiss as she pushed past. "Harrow sneakiness at its best." She paused for a few moments. "One of my cleaning staff overheard a conversation on the phone as she cleaned the room. Apparently, Ms. Doyle met someone at the diner in town for lunch. She remembers the conversation because of all the insults used."

Had to be Elspeth on the other end of the phone. Only one person in Point Muse could drive someone to so many insults in one conversation. "Thanks, Rose." Xandie turned to Lila. "We need to get to the diner and warn Bridget the killer is after her piece of the amulet."

"If they don't already have it."

And if the killer didn't? First stop, the diner and Bridget Doyle.

The killer is always one step ahead.

"I didn't touch the fortune-teller. Not my fault she's an overeater." Elspeth backed into the corner of the diner, arms folded over a non-existent chest as the healer worked on Bridget Doyle.

"She ate two blueberry pies, two lobster pies, and a plate of French fries. That's not just overeating, that's a death wish."

Xandie fought a gag as she stepped around blueberry-colored vomit.

"It ain't my food. The health department has

already cleared me this week." The diner's owner and cook crossed meaty arms over his stained shirt.

"That's a shock," Xandie mumbled to Lila.

"That flaky waitress of mine, Delilah, took sick halfway through her shift. I can't cook and clean too."

"Since when do you clean, Harold?" Elspeth sneered. "You're a sloth shifter. Laziness is your middle name."

"Now you look here, Elspeth Harrow, I'm not afraid of you." Harold shook his fist at the elderly witch.

Elspeth grinned, white dentures on show. "Really?" she purred and drew out the word as every lightbulb in the diner popped with a hiss, showering everyone in shards of glass.

"Elspeth, leash the hag," Buchanan bellowed as he strode in, quickly followed by Chief Braun and Agent Jackson.

Xandie's attention snagged on the brawny shifter. Only a little while ago, he'd thrown underwear at her and asked her on a date. She wasn't sure how to act around him now. The status quo of the Braun-Meyers squabbling had changed. She dropped her gaze down to poor Bridget and away from the shifter.

"I'll give you hag," Elspeth screeched back and gathered all the shadows in the diner around her like a medieval hooded cape. The only body part now visible was her amber Harrow eyes.

"At least we can see where she vacuum-sucked all the shadows to." Lila shrugged and scooted in next to Xandie and the late fortune-teller, Bridget Doyle.

The ex-coven member looked like she'd swum in blueberry pie, her skin colored in tie-dyed purple patterns. Xandie took a deep breath, put Braun out of her head, and knelt next to Bridget. A graveyard remnant of various foods surrounded the woman. Elspeth's nemesis had blue-tinged lips and a purple protruding tongue. But considering the amount of blueberry pie remains, the color could have been from that.

"She choked, I swear." Harold shuffled over to Xandie, wringing his hands. "She just kept shoveling food in and crying. She barely took time to swallow. I've never seen anything like it."

"Who was here at the time?" Maybe there were other witnesses she could interview who could clear Elspeth.

Harold rubbed a hand through sparse, stringy gray hair. "The lunch rush hasn't started. It was just those two old cacklers, me, and my waitress, Delilah. That good-for-nothing woman bailed halfway through her shift."

But Delilah wasn't a Morrigan Coven member, and she definitely wasn't at the top of Xandie's suspect list. That position was taken by Hellacious Whitburn.

"It was a gluttony hex." Elspeth stomped up and stared at the dead coven member with a loaded glance. "Bridget was an egotistical prima donna, happy to prostitute her gift, but she used to be a friend. She didn't deserve to die by shoveling food into her yap."

"And how do you know it's a gluttony hex, Ms. Harrow?" Agent Jackson leaned against the door-jamb as Braun and his deputies swarmed the room, along with Jackson's PIG agents.

Buchanan snorted. "How do you think? Elspeth may have a devious hag streak, but her hexes are pure genius."

Elspeth curtsied and winked at the grizzled Paladin agent. "Nice to see my skills appreciated."

"Compliments aside, a woman died by your hex. Try and show a little

sympathy." Lila rolled her eyes at her grand-mother's antics.

If Xandie didn't know better, she'd swear Elspeth was flirting with Buchanan. "Can we focus on the body and the fact that the killer could come for Elspeth next?"

"I can look after myself, granddaughter." Elspeth drew herself up, haughtiness in every inch of her demented diminutive frame.

Xandie nodded agreement. "You probably can, but the killer has how many pieces of the amulet now?"

Elspeth deflated. "Two. Henry and Bridget's. Mine and Lucien's are the last ones."

"Exactly. We need to get a step ahead of Whitburn."

Buchanan nodded. "I've got Paladins poring through his company and personal finances and past movements. He can't be working alone. He has to have an accomplice. I should have the information soon. That might give us an edge."

"But meanwhile..." Xandie narrowed her gaze on her grandmother. "Stay at Harrow House in full view of Buchanan and his leather-clad agents. No drugging and no escaping. Promise me?"

Braun snorted. "Good luck. Elspeth has a certain reputation amongst the unwary who take liquid refreshment from her." He stepped closer to Xandie.

"Speaking of liquid refreshment, have you decided on a time yet for our date?"

Jackson stepped forward. "Date? With him?" He used his metal wand to point at the shifter. "What about our nightcap?"

"Xandie?" Braun frowned.

For the love of... "Can we get Elspeth back to Harrow House and protection before I argue timings of dates?" *Whoops*, Xandie winced internally. That sounded suspiciously like she'd agreed to a date with Ethan Jackson as well. How did she get herself into these predicaments?

Holly broke in, trying to smooth the testosterone levels. "Not that she'd agreed to any after-hours dating with an agent from the Paranormal Investigative Group." She scowled at the agent. "Shame on you for taking advantage of the situation." Holly waggled her fingers warningly at Jackson, glaring like an old schoolteacher until the agent looked suitably chastened.

Jackson cleared his throat and changed the subject. "My bosses also have questions about the legalities of some of Elspeth Harrow's hexes."

"Great. It's a party." Elspeth cheered and clapped her hands. "I have this special pumpkin mimosa I want to try on you. It's to die for." Elspeth winked and then led a groaning pack of agents out of the diner.

Lila leaned into Xandie. "They're gonna wish she *had* hexed them."

Truer words were never spoken by a Harrow.

FOURTEEN

"I think you need this more than I do." Zach Braun waved a steaming takeaway cup in front of Xandie's face.

She opened one eye and squinted at the too-cheerful chief of police. "You're being nice. What do you want?"

Zach placed the honey-sweetened coffee in front of Xandie. "I heard about the karaoke competition last night. Who knew Buchanan could belt out show tunes?"

Xandie grabbed the coffee and sipped a mouthful, wincing as the honeyed caffeine hit the back of her throat. She preferred hot chocolate or a lovely milky tea, but when facing a killer and hung-over Harrows, the shot of caffeine would come in handy.

"Yeah, and who knew they'd carry on until three am. Good thing Harrow House is set away from our neighbors."

"At least Elspeth kept busy."

"Busy recording everyone else so she can blackmail them later."

"I wouldn't expect anything less from Elspeth Harrow." Braun paused and assessed Xandie. "How are you doing?"

"There's a killer stalking my grandmother, and those damn PIG agents waver between treating Elspeth as a future victim or the evil perpetrator, so I guess I'm as good as it's gonna get."

"Jackson disappeared quickly from the diner yesterday. Anyone would think he was embarrassed about being called out on something?"

"You'd have to talk to him. Actually, don't do that. You two have a tendency to dissolve into arguing." Xandie paused and licked her lips. They hadn't solved the Elspeth/coven issue yet, so their future date still loomed unresolved, but at least she could offer Zach an answer to one question. "Jackson asked for a nightcap after the poisoned milk incident. Once I found out the Paranormal Investigative Group had a file on me, I declined...*loudly*. I think he was trying to aggravate you."

"That's what PIG is good at. Paladin is a little more subtle about their manipulation." He smiled slowly and focused on Xandie. "So, no backing out?"

"Not unless you annoy me." Xandie drained her coffee and slammed it on the table. Thank goodness for beverages, caffeinated or otherwise. She actually felt halfway human again and somewhat awkward about this entire conversation.

Holly stumbled down the stairs, eyes half closed. "Do I smell coffee?"

Xandie shoved the empty takeaway cup at Zach. "Braun bought a honey coffee for himself, but he finished it. Try the coffee pot. Lila made some before she left for work."

Braun smirked at Xandie's lie. But after a night of off-key caterwauling, she wasn't about to admit to taking caffeine bribes from attractive law enforcement officers.

"I'll take anything right now. Those pumpkin mimosas leave a nasty morning aftertaste."

Elspeth sailed into the kitchen, bright-eyed, with a neon-blue, waist length curly wig flaring behind her. "Might be the wormwood I slipped into that last batch. I'll work on it."

"Why in all that is holy in Point Muse are you not hung over?" Holly glared at her grandmother.

Looking innocent, Elspeth shrugged. "Probably my black heart. You should try it sometime."

"Pass. We already have enough issues with our Harrow DNA," Holly whispered to Xandie. Both girls giggled until Elspeth frowned.

"Librarian, where are we with our investigation?" Elspeth deposited herself at the head of the dining table and nodded encouragingly.

Xandie cleared her throat. Where were they? Living in the land of bupkis with zero clues, but she couldn't tell Elspeth that. "Well, I mean..."

"Spit it out, child. Do I need to dose you with something?"

"Cease the evil witch routine, woman." Buchanan slapped a file on the table. "Whitburn's financials and history, contacts, even his bra size."

"Bra size?" Holly scratched her head, confused.

"He likes to wear disguises, apparently." Xandie focused back on the file scuffle between Elspeth and the Paladin.

Xandie released her held breath as Buchanan's file stole Elspeth's attention.

"Nice redirection from the Paladin," Braun whispered to Xandie.

His honey-scented breath tickled her ear. Xandie

refused to look at the police chief as Elspeth and Buchanan squabbled over who'd hold the file.

"Isn't everyone nice and cozy?" Agent Jackson slammed Harrow House's front door behind him.

"Look what the House let in." Elspeth sneered good-naturedly at Jackson.

"Can you tell me why I have three agents sick this morning?"

Xandie and Holly pointed straight at Elspeth without saying a word.

"Your boys couldn't handle the pumpkin mimosas or the karaoke. Not my fault."

"Our medic had to dose them with a cure-all potion before they stopped vomiting and seeing double."

"Might be time to look at employee standards." Elspeth winked. "But when has PIG ever had standards?"

"Ooh, zing. Elspeth—one. Agent—zilch." Theo wandered in with a hot pink wig askew on his head.

Everyone in the room stopped and stared at the fuzzy black cat.

"What? Never seen a talking cat in a pink wig before?"

"Oh, good gracious. What have you done,

Elspeth?" Holly pointed a trembling finger at the older woman.

Elspeth nodded in satisfaction. "I may have placed a tiny spell on Theo so he could sing aloud last night. His rendition of that Titanic song was epic. And he begged so beautifully, I couldn't resist making a few adjustments to his vocal cords. I still had some potion left after creating my baby boy, Colin."

"Yes, but you assured us it would wear off by the morning. That damn talking pug of yours is bad enough. Until now, only Xandie had to suffer Theo's mouthy comments. We were fine with that. We don't need more talking animals in Harrow House."

Xandie rolled her eyes at the look of horror on her cousin's face. None of Theo's or her grandmother's antics were a surprise to her. Everyone else could hear her cat's voice now, not just her. Not to mention his complaints ad nauseam. Until now, Xandie had been the only one to hear Theo because of his link to the Library. But now everybody else had to suffer. *Suckers.*

"Yep, watch out, witches. Theo's rapping in da house." The cat pranced around the kitchen, wiggling his tail before pouncing on a dust ball and wrestling it into submission.

Buchanan snatched the file out of Elspeth's hands. "Mind if we focus on Whitburn's financials before another dead body appears?"

"The Paranormal Investigative Group has already run Whitburn's finances. There's nothing of interest here."

"And we're going to trust the group that let Whitburn slip through their fingers to begin with? No offense, but I'm happy to trust Paladin info over anything you're likely to come up with any day." Braun crossed his arms over his chest and glowered.

"I'm sure as local law enforcement, you have valid insight into Point Muse, but the group is more accustomed to dealing with bigger issues."

"In other words, Zachy bear, he doesn't think you should play with the big boys. Maybe he's jealous you scored coffee time with our single Librarian." Theo hacked up the dust ball he'd accidentally swallowed and batted it at the agent's boots.

Buchanan snorted. "I think Paladin has both you boys beat since we deal with worldwide mass magic extinction events."

Elspeth rolled her eyes. "For Hecate's sake, put your manly egos away. It pains me to admit it, but you're all big enough to play in Point Muse." Elspeth snatched the file from Buchanan's grasp and scanned the contents. "Whitburn's video game company has been steadily bleeding profits for the last five years. Our wealthy necromancer is on the verge of bankruptcy. Then six months ago, he disappeared from public view, and his vice president is now running the shop."

What happened six months ago to send Whitburn into hiding? Xandie leaned forward and tapped the table. "It's not the money. Something must have sent him into hiding, or at least out of view. What was it? Was PIG monitoring him?"

Jackson took a seat at the table, all macho posturing forgotten. "As long as he completed his mandatory check-in, we weren't interested in him. Considered him low risk."

"And that's where we differ, boyo. Paladin thinks Whitburn is a loose cannon. We've kept a semiregular surveillance team on the necromancer since Elspeth contacted us initially with her suspicions on Proctor during World War Two. In fact, all members of the Morrigan Coven have been under surveillance."

Elspeth snorted, and Buchanan amended his statement. "Almost all the coven. This old hag has a habit of blocking our surveillance. We only check in with her occasionally now."

"Back to six months ago. What was Whitburn doing?" The necromancer disappearing for no reason annoyed Xandie's orderly brain. They were missing something.

Elspeth flipped through the file. "He was approaching banks to bail out his company. Most froze him out until one institution backed him, but he turned them down flat. Said he didn't need the money anymore."

Bingo. Somehow, he'd come into money, but from where? "That's it. That's what we're missing. Check the surveillance around then. Who was in contact with him?"

Buchanan snapped his fingers and nodded at Xandie. "You're on the right track, Meyers. Hang on." He snatched the file back from a hissing Elspeth and grabbed the phone records. "In a four-week period leading up to that date, he received multiple phones calls every few days from a burner phone."

"Paladin Inc. didn't find that curious?" Jackson tweaked a supercilious smile at the older man.

"An investigation was started. Then it was determined that Whitburn had engaged in phone and escort duties with a contractual supernatural dating service. My agents checked out the service, and they confirmed Whitburn had scheduled phone interactions with an employee named Alberta. No last name of record."

And there it was. *Alberta.* "That's the same name as the person who's been organizing the tickets for the singles' cruise and getting people out of the way. Alberta, whoever she is, is Whitburn's accomplice."

"Lookee there, big boys. Seems like my Librarian granddaughter found a clue you all missed." Elspeth cackled and slapped the table, her mirth causing her dentures to wobble back and forth.

Tearing her eyes away from the mesmerizing effect, Xandie ignored her grandmother. "The big issue is who initiated the contact first? We're assuming Whitburn is the bad guy leader. What happens if he's just an errand boy?"

"Whitburn identifies with a strong female lead, but I suspect he groomed this Alberta as a potential henchwoman from first contact. Our focus should be Whitburn primarily." Jackson took out a notepad and made a few notations. "Ms. Harrow and the vampire, Benoit, are our priority now. With all the amulets, Whitburn could force a supernatural panic across the world that would bring entire countries to their knees."

Braun stiffened next to Xandie as his phone

vibrated.

Xandie whispered to him as he fumbled it out. "Let me guess. Elspeth spelled your phone so you can get better reception?"

He grunted an affirmation before grabbing his phone and heading into the hallway.

Since when did Braun need privacy? Maybe something was afoot? Xandie shoved Braun out of her head for the moment and looked around the room. "Where's Benoit?"

Elspeth wrinkled her nose and checked the time. "He left about an hour ago with two PIG agents to do a bakery run. He should have been back by now."

"We've got a problem." Braun strode into the room with a worried grimace, along with a furry monobrow covering his forehead. "Benoit never made it to the bakery. A pack of dead animals ran them off the road, and an elemental hex incapacitated the two agents. Trees along the side of the road had them tied up as soon as they exited the car. The vampire's missing and presumed injured as they found blood on the passenger seat."

That meant Whitburn had the third piece of the amulet, but it would take time to cut the tattoo out and transmute it back into its solid state.

Then it's Elspeth's turn...

FIFTEEN

"Looks like the human cavalry twigged to a potential supernatural Armageddon."

"Huh?" Xandie looked up as her cousin, Lila, slumped into a chair next to her.

"The black-suited agents have me run off my feet." Lila indicated the empty bakery cabinet.

Xandie finally noticed the group of men crowding into Lila's bakery. Black suits, *check*. Military haircuts, *check*. Annoying, supercilious expressions, *check*. ASP was in Point Muse. She'd run into the Anti-Species Project a few times over the last few months, but since the incidents in the parking garage of the hospital and the pet show, they'd kept their distance. Now the threat of supernatural

Armageddon had bought the ASP agents out in force.

"Told you I'd see you again, Meyers."

The gravelly voice she recognized ripped at her nerve endings. The overzealous agent who'd threatened her at the hospital *and* the cocktail party at the pet show stood smoking a cigarette in front of her. "I'd love to say it's great to see you again, but I'd be lying."

The golden dragons handled the removal of this joker for her when Marjorie Penne had been in a coma. And Xandie had put him in his place at the cocktail party. She'd hoped he'd gotten the message that his presence wasn't wanted in Point Muse, but here he was, with his regular buzz cut and black suit, still in her face. He must want her mom, Miranda Harrow, so badly.

"ASP will always look over your shoulder. You and that Harrow family are on our radar."

"Yeah, but is my mother? Weren't you looking for her, not so long ago? Did you find her?"

"Your mother will come in soon. She won't be able to help herself when she remembers her darling daughter. Just because Miranda Harrow's protected by the big dogs now doesn't mean she always will be."

Big dogs? What was the ASP ass talking about?

"Miranda's alive?" Elspeth stood in the doorway. Black clouds literally hovered above her head.

Xandie clenched her teeth. The last thing she needed right now was Elspeth Harrow on an emotional rampage.

The ASP agent let out a bark of laughter. "What a surprise. The Harrows are keeping secrets. The apple doesn't fall far from the tree with you three, does it?"

Xandie took a deep breath as the agent dropped his bombshell and left with a gaggle of other agents.

Lila moved cups and plates out of reach of Xandie and Elspeth.

"I'm not going to snap and throw your serving plates."

"I'm not worried about you." Lila pointed to Elspeth as she weaved a path to Xandie. The black clouds wreathed her body with mini flashes of lightning.

"Granddaughter? Got something to tell me?" Elspeth rose into the air, her clouds holding her in place, her now snowy white wig streaming out behind her.

Family drama, the cornerstone of Harrow life. "Look, Great-Aunt Sera started investigating Mom's disappearance. Her troll private investigator found a

Merrow witness. Twenty years ago, Mom was alive but had no memory of her past life or us. Those ASP idiots swept in and snatched her. That's all I know. But now she's missing again, and they're looking for her too." Xandie threw her hands in the air as tiny electrical sparks flickered over the table where her hands had just rested.

"Where is she?"

"I told you, ASP lost her. I think she might be getting some of her memories back and has gone rogue. Because when Marjorie Penne was in a coma, they tried to use me as bait to get her back. A golden dragon stepped in and got rid of them. Since then, the agents have periodically popped up. But mostly, they keep their distance. They come just close enough to let me know they're there."

The clouds thinned out around Elspeth, and she dropped to the ground with a thump. "I understand not telling the rest of my offspring. But why keep it a secret from your grandmother?"

"Because it's still only reports, rumors. Nothing verifiable or concrete." Xandie sighed and looked forlornly at Elspeth. "I didn't want to get *my* hopes up, let alone yours."

Elspeth considered Xandie's words and then slapped the table and sat. "Fair enough. But next time you keep a secret like that..." Elspeth drew a line across the base of her throat and cackled, but there was no energy in it.

"I have a question." Lila held a hand up like she was a schoolgirl. "What did that ASP mean when he talked about Miranda being protected by the big dogs?"

Nodding, Elspeth pursed her lips. "Excellent point. If someone's protecting her from the government, they have to have a power base to back it up. There are only two legitimate choices in the supernatural world. The Paranormal Investigative Group and Paladin Inc."

Xandie shook her head, confused. "Surely both groups would have notified us when they realized who she was."

"Depends on how useful Miranda was to them," Elspeth sneered. "PIG will use you until you're useless and then discard you. Paladin always has an angle for the greater good and all that pious poop."

"You said *two legitimate choices*. So, we're talking about *above board entities*. But what about the not so legal ones?" Lila chimed in.

"Well..." Elspeth dragged the word out as a gleam appeared in her eyes. "There are a few private consortiums that would have the juice to keep

Miranda hidden, but no one would dare cross me. I'll put some feelers out, but my best bet is those two law enforcement losers already in town."

"Let me guess. Elspeth's spewing her anti-Paladin views again?" Buchanan scrambled over Lila's bakery counter and stood with a heaving chest as he scowled at the elder witch.

"I'm equal opportunity. I hate the PIGs as well." She traded scowl for scowl.

"Next time you raise a metaphysical barrier around the bakery, you might reinforce the back door. It only took me ten minutes to break through."

Elspeth smiled, a wicked slash of dentures. "You mean when I let you in?"

"Listen here, hag. I'm your protective detail. I'm trying to keep your wrinkled patootie alive."

"Ain't no wrinkles here, honey." Elspeth patted her bottom planted in Lila's chair.

"Timeout, please." Xandie did a hand signal above her head. "No one needs to imagine Elspeth's rear end. Besides, don't we have more important issues at stake? Like dead bodies, missing vampires, pending Armageddon, and missing mothers?"

In a move that belied her elderly years, Elspeth stomped up to Buchanan and pointed an accusing finger. "Speaking of missing mothers, where is my Miranda, you daughter thief?"

"Have you been at your potions again, Harrow? Your daughter died years ago."

Xandie cleared her throat. "*About that...* According to ASP, she had memory loss after her fall, and they acquired her at the hospital. She worked for them until she disappeared. The agent implied Paladin or the PIGs have her now."

Buchanan frowned. "I've been on non-active status for the last ten years until this Morrigan Coven incident. If it's need to know, I wouldn't be on the list." He stared at Elspeth, somber. "If I'd known, I would have told you straight away. Your family doesn't deserve to lose anyone else."

Elspeth patted the grizzled Paladin on a whiskered cheek. "I know. But we need to find Miranda before the government does."

Buchanan covered Elspeth's hand with his own. "I'll call in some favors. If she's out there, we'll find her."

Lila leaned in and fake whispered to break the tension filling the bakery. "Is this an episode of old people falling in love?"

Elspeth whipped around and pointed a finger at her granddaughter. "I think Lila Harrow would look grand with an extra nose, don't you? It would remind her to keep her noses out of my business."

Lila covered her face and dropped to the floor behind Xandie. "You wouldn't risk hitting your favorite Librarian granddaughter, would you?"

"Are you really using me as an Elspeth cover, Lila? Where's your family loyalty?" Xandie scooted out of the way and exposed Lila to Elspeth, the angst of dealing with ASP and her grandmother forgotten in the wake of Harrow antics.

"Pfft." Elspeth snapped her fingers. "It's not worth it. Not when she's expecting it. I'll wait until everything dies down. The fear of the unexpected is much more satisfying."

"Are we done here?" Buchanan growled at the bakery in general and maneuvered Elspeth out the door. "We need to get back to Harrow House ASAP. It's too open here."

Xandie followed her grandmother and her Paladin bodyguard but stopped to throw a wicked grin at Lila. "I think you better buy some big floppy hats to hide your noses, because your goose is cooked, cousin."

With a cheerful wave, Xandie stepped outside onto Main Street. She lifted her face to the patchy sun and inhaled slowly. Winter was around the corner, and although Point Muse was on the main coast and temperatures weren't as extreme as in other parts of Maine, snow still fell. The vamps would be out in force as winter brought on the darker days.

Xandie stiffened as her shoulder blades itched. Pivoting, she stared at both ends of Main Street, searching for shadowy ASP agents stalking her. But the black-suited government men had disappeared from the streets of Point Muse. With a frown on her face, she jogged to catch up to her grandmother and Buchanan.

Giving into impulse, she rubbed the back of the neck as she sidestepped a group of witchy tourists standing there gossiping. Something didn't feel right. She stopped and swung around without warning, hoping to catch someone watching. A shadowy figure stepped back into an alley between an empty store and Aunt Winifred's candle shop. Xandie froze. The prickling on her neck exploded and sent needles along her nerve endings.

"Something picking at your craw, granddaughter?" Elspeth slid next to Xandie and peered at her face. "You okay, little Xandie?"

Xandie forced a smile and turned back to her grandmother, linking arms with her. "I'm fine. Just an imp walking over my grave." She led Elspeth back to Buchanan but risked a quick glance over her shoulder. The alley was empty of anything resembling either a government agent or a stalking, shadowy figure, but someone *had* been watching her. She'd stake her life on it.

But friend or foe?

SIXTEEN

"I found it. I found the link." Holly ran down the steps of Harrow House, flapping a file overhead.

Elspeth slammed the door to Buchanan's nondescript SUV. "What are you wailing about, Death Girl?"

Holly glared at her grandmother. "I found new information that might help. But if you keep calling me Death Girl, I'll bury it out back, and you'll never find it."

"Fine. Holly, my second favorite granddaughter, what momentous news have you found for us?"

Holly flapped the files overhead again. "Albert Proctor had a second child."

What? Xandie stepped up to her triumphant

cousin and grabbed the file, flipping through it. "According to Holly's information, Proctor had an illegitimate child who'd been adopted out."

Elspeth sagged against Buchanan. "We only knew of one child. That boy who exploded Paladin headquarters."

Right, Proctor's son. He killed Elspeth's husband and Xandie's grandfather and decimated the Paladin power structure. The same group who'd allowed Elspeth's investigation into Proctor. "The illegitimate child would have been older than the son by a few years."

Holly nodded. "The adoption records are sealed, but the baby's name on her birth certificate was Alberta."

"Named for her father, Albert." Elspeth pushed away from Buchanan.

"And the same name as the woman giving way all those free cruise tickets to get people out of town." Xandie gave Holly the file back and patted her shoulder. "Way to go, cousin. You found information. Both the Paladins and the PIGs found zip."

"I'd resent that statement, but unfortunately, it's accurate." PIG agent Ethan Jackson stepped onto the front porch of Harrow House, phone in hand.

"Thanks to Holly's information, we have linked the Alberta from the supernatural agency to the one in the adoption file."

"So, Whitburn deliberately hunted this Alberta down after coming across the adoption file?" He'd recruited a woman who'd never turn on him because of a hatred for the woman instrumental in the investigation of Morrigan Coven and ultimately her father's death.

"That's what we suspect." Jackson waggled the phone at Xandie. "Phone call for you. Some Troll."

Her great-aunt's private investigator, Herman. Xandie ran up the stairs and snatched the phone from the Forget-Me-Witch agent. "Herman?"

"How you doing, Librarian girl?"

Xandie hip-shoved Jackson toward Elspeth and Holly before turning back to Harrow House. "Surviving, Herman, surviving. Any good news for me?" Xandie leaned against the open front door and watched Buchanan and Jackson squabble about their next move.

"Someone's been applying pressure to the backers behind ASP. There are mumblings about dodgy dealings and illegal activities by both the backers of ASP and their agents. Word is someone high in Paladin is putting the smack-down on ASP. Looks like the government is listening so far. Most of their agents are being recalled to headquarters."

Could the big dog protecting her mother be Paladin, not PIG? "Any information on my mom?"

Herman cleared his throat. "This is unofficial, and my source won't go on record. She assures me Miranda Harrow is alive and well."

"But where is she?" Xandie clenched the phone tight. Her mother was okay, but she still wasn't standing close enough to hug. Frustration gnawed on Xandie's nerves.

"Considering the large contingency of ASP agents still hiding in Point Muse, despite their orders, I'm betting she ain't far away."

In a perfect world, her mother would be just around the corner. But Point Muse wasn't perfect. The body count proved that.

"Thanks for your help, Herman. Keep me updated."

"My invoice is in the mail. I'll call you if anything else comes up. Be safe, Librarian."

Xandie bit her lip as Herman hung up. "Yes, safe. In Point Muse." She lifted her eyes to the heavens and whispered a plea for good luck. As she stared up, a black speck soared above their heads, circling around Harrow House. She squinted as the bird moved closer. It looked like a falcon. Peregrine falcons loved Point Muse and nested heavily throughout the area.

Holly followed Xandie's gaze as the bird soared above them.

Elspeth stepped between the warring law enforcement agents as the bird circled back, right overhead.

The falcon dropped in height, low enough Xandie could make out the blue-gray helmet that covered its head and face and its white feathered throat...*and* the sizeable chunks of skin missing from its lower body.

A zombie falcon. The bird folded its wings in and fell into a sharp vertical dive. Right at Elspeth and the agents. Xandie leapt forward, screaming a warning.

Holly picked up on the danger and dragged Elspeth out of the way, leaving the agents to stare at the Harrow women in shock.

The falcon reared back, claws extended and its beak open at an impossible angle. The bird was in attack mode and probably loaded with one of

Elspeth's heinous hexes. And no one was clear of the fallout zone.

A slim, hooded figure strode out of the tree line to the side of Harrow House and raised something to its shoulder. The figure paused for a moment, as if sighting the bird and, with no noise or vibration, launched a projectile into the feathered attacker. It ignited in a greenish-blue flame until nothing was left but ash that floated down on the light breeze.

Xandie ran forward, but Elspeth yanked her back.

"See that green flame?" Elspeth pointed to the green fire that lingered in the air, even though the body had turned to ash and had now drifted away. "When that...whoever it was... shot that diseased bird, I think it was ready to let loose one of my radioactive belches. But the bird imploded instead. That flame is the leftover radioactive hex in the air. You don't want to go near it."

Xandie stared at the slim, mid-height shooter. From a distance, it was impossible to tell whether they were male or female, but something in Xandie's gut screamed female. The shooter raised a hand, and Elspeth choked up behind Xandie.

Her grandmother's hand tightened like claws on Xandie's arms, holding her in place. "Stay."

"That's..." She couldn't finish the thought, her words failing her.

"The only person in our family other than my husband who was an excellent shot with a bow and a gun. Mystical or physical, your mother and your grandfather were expert shots." Elspeth dropped her hands away from Xandie as the figure disappeared back into the tree line.

She rounded on her grandmother. "If that was my mother, why hold me back?"

"We don't know how much she remembers. Miranda could be operating on instinct. A wounded animal can be very dangerous when cornered. We wait for her to approach us."

Xandie closed her eyes for a moment. She knew her grandmother was right, but the temptation to run after Miranda Harrow beat at her resolve. "Fine. What do you suggest we do?"

Elspeth jiggled her hipflask. "I think I need a top-up and those two need a timeout." She pointed to the still warring agents.

Xandie grabbed the back of Jackson's shirt and pulled him away from the older agent. "I'm glad Braun isn't here, otherwise the testosterone levels would choke us." She dropped her grasp after she'd shoved the agent back up the porch.

"And apparently you're dating the shifter, so his testosterone levels must appeal," Jackson growled and dusted himself off.

"My choice of date and his level of testosterone is none of your business. What is *your* business is how you conduct interagency cooperation."

"That Paladin is so frustrating..."

"Takes one to know one." Elspeth sailed past the aggrieved agent and into Harrow House.

Holly and Buchanan crowded up onto the porch, and everyone gaped at the suddenly cheery witch.

"Did she defend me?" Buchanan stared open-mouthed at Elspeth.

Holly shuddered. "Don't ask that...*ever*. If Xandie defended you, there's a reason. A diabolical, soul-destroying reason. Just go with it. It's better than facing eternal damnation." She stepped into the doorway of Harrow House. "Well, it's dinnertime somewhere in the world. Let's eat."

The trio crowded in behind Holly and followed her to the kitchen where Elspeth banged plates around.

"Did I see who I thought I saw?" Holly whispered.

"That's what Elspeth thinks. She also said Mom might be a wounded animal and not to approach."

"As much as it hurts me to agree with my evil grandmother, she's right. You don't know what Miranda remembers. She could see you as a threat."

Dammit, why did the Harrows always have to be right? Xandie huffed and dropped into a kitchen chair next to the old, battered table.

"Make yourself useful, girls." Elspeth dumped a container of cold cuts and a knife on the table. "Slice the meat up for dinner, and there's steamed cabbage, carrots, and potatoes in the refrigerator. Just needs heating."

Holly scowled at Elspeth. "Where are you disappearing to now?"

Elspeth sniffed dramatically. "The house needs my opinion on something. Plus, I need to change my wig. It clashes with the chocolate banana cream pie that's in the fridge for dessert."

Buchanan stood as Elspeth took a few steps. She whirled back and pointed an accusing finger. "Don't you dare, Patrick Buchanan. I am quite capable of picking my wig out. The house will keep an eye on me." She spun and stomped out.

Colin raised his head from a large embroidered gold pillow placed in the corner of the room. "Her wigs are her pride and joy. Even my bootylicious canine magnificence doesn't step into her room for fear of hex consequences. Bet that cat wouldn't care. In fact, send him in. He can be cannon fodder."

Speaking of Theo... "Where is my mouthy cat?" Xandie frowned at Colin. "Please tell me you didn't do something nefarious to him?"

"I can neither deny nor confirm that the annoying fake feline is glued to Elspeth's closet door." Colin shook himself, all his rolls wobbling in hypnotic coordination.

"Ignore the animal situation. We need Elspeth here, ASAP." Buchanan sat and glared at the PIG agent.

Jackson raised his hands in denial. "I have nothing to do with the animals, so don't glare at me. And it's not my issue what wig Ms. Harrow picks as long as she stays alive while doing it."

"Did I hear Elspeth mention chocolate cream pie earlier?" Holly opened the fridge and clapped like a little girl in delight.

"Elspeth's banana chocolate pie. I have no clue whether she baked or waggled her nose and used magic, but I'm saving room for a very large serving." Holly shut the fridge door and smiled at the room. "Now whose turn was it to fight?"

Xandie ignored the drama, piled the meat on a platter, and busied herself heating the vegetables.

Say what you will about her grandmother's anti-social tendencies, she knew how to feed a person.

Holly helped Xandie carry the dishes to the table. "Right. Someone go and drag Elspeth away from her wigs. Xandie, you need to deal with Harrow House." Holly pointed to Buchanan and Jackson. "You boys need to cool it before Elspeth threatens you with a hex."

The men grabbed plates and loaded food on.

What did she need to help Harrow House with? Harrow witches built the house over two hundred years ago. Various generations added on and improved it. And magic had built up within the walls until the house had become a sentient, protective Harrow guardian. And it had distinctive mood swings like a certain Harrow witch. A noisy banging echoed from the front of the house. Xandie jerked in shock as the noise rang out again.

"The front door's flapping. Means someone's coming, or the house wants to talk on the porch." Holly shrugged, unconcerned. "Or the zombie apocalypse is upon us again. Who knows?"

Sighing, Xandie headed for the door. She stepped outside onto the porch. "What's up, House? Don't tell me Elspeth hexed the whole town from her bedroom?"

The entire house quivered. Xandie grabbed a porch column and held on until the movement subsided. "That can't be a good omen."

A growling noise of mechanical engines along the Harrow driveway snapped Xandie to attention. "That's why. Someone not so nice is approaching the house. Someone on Elspeth's hex-on-sight list?"

The house vibrated again in response. "I'll take that as a yes," Xandie mumbled as three black SUVs rolled into sight and came to a dirt-spinning halt in front of Harrow House. The same black tinted vehicles those idiotic ASP agents paraded around town in. Her mother may have made an appearance and now the rogue agency hunting her head had as well.

The front door to Harrow House slammed open with a bang, and Holly stood framed in the doorway, her eyes wide. She stuttered a few words before clearing her throat and trying again, "We have a gigantic problem."

Xandie pointed to the three cars and the black-suited agents swarming onto Harrow land. "Yep. It's called ASP."

"Nope." Holly shook her head as men bellowing in unison drifted out of the house. "It's worse than that."

"Nothing's worse than egotistic, power-mad

human agents, bent on controlling all supernatural creatures, conducting a house call."

"Elspeth's missing."

"Right. We're now at DEFCON three."

A missing Elspeth was like a nuke on the loose.

Harrow help Point Muse if anyone got in her way...

SEVENTEEN

"Well, well. I told you I'd be seeing you soon, little Librarian." The head ASP agent with a graying military style buzz cut smiled at Xandie.

"And I told you I have no clue where Miranda Harrow is."

"There was a sighting of a woman who matches your mother's description not far from here."

And wouldn't this idiotic covert wannabe love to haul Xandie and her mother away to some sealed black ops site. No chance. "Afraid I can't help you. Plus, you're on private property without a warrant or permission. It's time for you to leave."

The agent leaned against his SUV and folded his arms over his chest. "This is a nice place you

Harrows have here. I think I might stay. Got any spare rooms?"

"From what I hear, you'll be out of a job soon, anyway. Time for a holiday?" Xandie smirked and thanked the gossip gods for her private investigator troll, Herman, and his sources.

The smile dropped away, and his beady eyes laser focused on Xandie. "Where did you hear that?"

"Around." Her troll was the secret ace up her proverbial sleeve. So, nameless, he would remain.

"ASP performs a necessary evil. We get rid of the supernatural vermin, like you and your family." The lead agent spat on the ground, and the other men formed a semicircle around him.

"Still sporting that same old prejudice, Malcolm?" Buchanan and Agent Jackson stood on the porch with their hands braced on their hips while Holly hovered in the doorway.

"I'm a patriot, Buchanan. You wouldn't understand."

"And I'm hungry and the sun's starting to set. Can anyone say kebabs?" Zach Braun strode out from behind Harrow House, followed by his deputy brothers. He came to a stop next to Xandie and scratched his nose with a sharp, gleaming bear claw.

Nodding to his men to withdraw, the ASP agent

opened his car door but paused and stared at Xandie. "Miranda Harrow is ours. No matter who pulls our strings. She'll always belong to ASP." He slammed the door shut, and all the vehicles reversed out of sight, in a spray of dirt and gravel.

"Shame. I was a bit peckish." Braun smirked at Xandie and retracted his bear claws. He frowned when she failed to respond. "What's wrong?"

"Other than the fact there's a murderer on the loose, a prejudiced government agent stalking my mother, and my grandmother seems to have disappeared again? Nothing."

Every person in Xandie's vicinity paled, and a few curse words drifted on the breeze. She nodded grimly. A disappearing Elspeth was bad enough. But Elspeth on a hunt was even worse.

***

"We need to get out of here and find Elspeth," Holly whispered to Lila and Xandie.

"How? Those damn ASP agents are everywhere now in Point Muse. Not to mention all the Paladin and PIG agents on the lookout for Harrows. Besides, where do we start?" Lila shifted on her seat and pretended to stretch as she looked around the dining room in Harrow House.

"We need a diversion," Xandie hissed and then smiled sweetly at Braun, Buchanan, and Jackson who all stared at the women suspiciously. "And I think I have an idea where she might have gone."

"For those of us without Librarian brains, would you care to share?" Lila coughed to cover her words.

"The killer has been one step ahead of us all along. We know that Hellacious has been working with a female. The same woman getting key people out of town with that cruise."

"And?" This time, Holly coughed.

"Whitburn and his partner are watching us. I think they want Elspeth off kilter, upset. They want her to make mistakes. They'll force her to meet them in the one area near Point Muse that will hurt her the most. Where the killer knight chased my mom off the cliff. I think that's where they'll be waiting."

Xandie pretended to have a fit of coughing. They needed to escape the house and get out to the bluff before Elspeth did something they'd all regret. *And* before Whitburn got his hands on the last piece of the Morpheus Amulet. But first, they needed to shake their law enforcement bodyguards. It'd be better if they didn't interfere in whatever plan Elspeth had going on.

"Somehow, I don't think you're getting a cold. So, how about you just tell me what you're plotting?" Buchanan growled.

Lila stood. "Sorry, girls. I agree with them. We need to let the agents handle this." She turned her back on the men and gave her cousins a large wink.

This had the hallmark signs of a Lila Harrow diversion. Xandie grabbed Holly's hand under the table and squeezed.

Holly jiggled her hand, acknowledging Xandie's sign.

"What? You sugar addicted traitor! What happened to all the Harrows standing together?" Holly jumped up and shoved Lila.

"I'm looking out for you and Elspeth, you death-loving lunatic." Lila tripped Holly over and danced around like a prize-winning boxer.

Braun wandered over to Xandie and leaned in close. "Just ask Harrow House to keep Buchanan and Jackson in. But you need to let me know where to send the troops for your back-up."

His honey-scented breath tickled her nape. His warm, solid shifter body pressed against her side. Damn bear had a way of discombobulating her. *Fine, deal it is.* "The bluff where my mother fell from. Just tell your men to stay out of the way until we signal. We don't want them caught in Elspeth's crossfire," she whispered to Braun while Jackson and Buchanan were pulling Lila and Holly apart.

Braun nodded and straightened. "Thanks for the show, ladies, but Xandie needs your help in the hallway. She needs to find a map to see where Elspeth might have gone." He grabbed the women by the elbows and pointed them toward Xandie. "Right, boys. I got a plan in place."

Holly and Lila scuttled over to where Xandie now hovered in the hallway near the front stairs.

"Now, House." Xandie snapped her fingers, and the house's frame quivered before a solid wall slid over the dining room opening, closing the agents in. "Let them free when it's time or when Braun tells you to, House. Thank you." Xandie patted a wall.

"What just happened?" Holly frowned, confused. "I thought our diversion was going well." She shook a fist at Lila. "I had a really good right hook ready for you."

"Looks to me like our little Xandie is in cahoots with the bear shifter. Is this a prelude to your coffee date?" Lila squinted at Xandie. "What's gotten into you? I know I was encouraging you, but you haven't even gone on that date yet and you're collaborating with the fuzz? It would devastate Elspeth."

Xandie spluttered. "He knows Elspeth is our best bet. *And our craziest liability.* She'll spook if she sees all the law enforcement agents. His men have orders to wait until we signal. That was the best compromise I could make. Our focus is Elspeth and getting all the pieces of the Morpheus Amulet."

Elspeth would have conniptions if Xandie dated a policeman, even a bear shifter one. But it wasn't like she was planning a future with him...*right?*

Lila shrugged. "Right. That's all I needed. Everyone into the bakery van. We have a supernatural apocalypse to stop and a crazy grandmother to protect."

The apocalypse was the easier task.

EIGHTEEN

"Why did we have to park a marathon length away again? My calves are killing me."

"Maybe you should lay off your own sweets, Baker Girl?"

"Could you two be quiet? I'm trying to concentrate." Xandie squinted. It was dark, but between the mostly full moon and Holly's banshee eyes, which flickered silver every few minutes, they could see enough to walk.

"I'm just saying, we could have gotten a little closer. Saved some time." Lila rubbed her calf muscle.

"We need to check the situation out before dropping in on Elspeth's scheme." The cliffs where her mother disappeared weren't far away. From now on, they had to keep a sharp eye out. Who knew what Hellacious and his female partner had planned?

A low moaning somewhere to Xandie's left froze her.

"Did anyone else hear that?" Lila stopped and gripped Holly, pushing her in front.

"Why am I the meat shield?" Holly wailed.

"Because you deal with dead things all the time, that's why."

"I think moaning's a good indication of life." Xandie hushed her cousins and concentrated. The whimper came again, only a few yards away. "This way." Xandie took point cautiously. The whimper sounded again, coming from the foot of a large red oak tree. "There." Xandie pointed to a shadowy, crumpled form at the base.

Taking a chance, she sped up. Whoever was moaning needed help. She knelt next to the figure and slowly rolled the body over into the moonlight. The missing Lucien Benoit, vampire and ex-Morrigan Coven member, and Elspeth's crony. "It's Elspeth's vampire, and he's still alive but hurt badly."

Holly and Lila pressed in next to Xandie. Holly quickly ripped off his shirt and exposed the gaping wound in his upper chest. She tore strips from his shirt and pressed them against the wound. Lucien squealed and sagged against the ground, unconscious. "It's not life threatening, but he needs blood and a good healer. A silver knife was used to cut out the amulet tattoo. Vamps' systems don't like silver, so the wounds take longer to heal."

Hellacious had Benoit's amulet piece. She had no choice but to go on, leaving Holly and Lila to help the vampire. Elspeth would never forgive them otherwise. "Lila, you need to grab the van, pick up Holly and the vampire, and get them to a healer."

"What about you?" Lila bit her lip, torn between keeping the vampire alive and staying with her cousin.

"I've got Elspeth somewhere out there with an evil plan. Plus, Theo got into the Library, and he's monitoring the situation. He'll let Harrow House know when it's time to send in the troops. He'll get Braun ready to go, so get out of here." Xandie patted Benoit's uninjured shoulder and stood. She had no doubt her errant mother was lurking in the shadows, watching. Whether Miranda Harrow remembered them was another story. She'd helped them once, and Xandie had to hope she'd do it again.

With a nod goodbye, Xandie followed the almost non-existent path to the bluff. She sped up as bushes rustled to her left and a high-pitched panting noise came from behind her. She came to a full stop, hands outstretched, ready to fake karate chop anything that came her way.

"Geez, doll face. If I'd known it was a hike, I'd have rethought this whole rescuing the damsel in distress plan." Colin stumbled out and dropped to the ground, rolling into his back as he wiggled his paws in relief.

"Colin? What on earth are you doing? And since when has Elspeth been a damsel in distress? She's more likely to be the wicked witch." Great, the mouthy pug wasn't her picture of a warrior riding to Elspeth's rescue. He made too much noise for anything covert.

"She is wicked, but everyone needs a helping paw every so often." Colin rolled over and pushed himself up. "I'm ready for my rescue attempt now."

His? "You mean my rescue plan?"

"Yeah, yeah. Same difference. Tally ho." Colin trotted off to the right.

Xandie cleared her throat. "Back this way."

"Right. What's the plan then, Library Girl?"

"Get Elspeth and the amulet and try not to get killed?" *Hopefully.*

"Short and sweet, like me."

Xandie slapped a hand over her nose as a low

rumble sounded from in front of her. "Can't you keep it in until we get to the bluff? We might be able to use your stench as a weapon."

"Hey," Colin objected. "I have stomach issues. But that time, it wasn't me."

The noise came again, accompanied by a stench of garbage as a white-tailed deer with a dented side pulled out from the bushes. On the other side, a gray fox with patches of peeling fur gave a sharp yip.

Hellacious Whitburn's creepy animal necromancy was herding her and Colin with dead animals. Xandie shuddered but forced herself onward. She had no choice, Elspeth needed her.

Xandie and the pug broke through the underbrush out onto a flat cliff. The same cliff where a killer knight chased her mother to her supposed death. Xandie shuddered, her hands moist, crazy imps turning cartwheels in her stomach.

"I'm sorry, Ms. Meyers. Truly sorry."

Xandie turned in the direction of the lisping male voice, noticing that despite his bulk and radioactive flatulence, Colin had slipped away undetected.

"I never wanted to hurt anyone, but she gave me no choice." A disheveled, cadaver-like Hellacious Whitburn stood to her right. Close to the cliff edge.

He looked worse for wear. Clothing torn in places, his black shoulder-length hair greasy and knotted. His skin sagged in places where he'd lost too much weight too quickly.

"Hellacious Whitburn, I presume?"

He nodded in a jerky, robotic fashion. "Tell Elspeth it wasn't personal. It was all her, Proctor's daughter."

"Killing your coven members wasn't personal?" Yeah, keep telling yourself that, psycho necromancer. And denial was a river in Egypt as Elspeth would say.

"No, no. Not me." Hellacious started for a moment. "She knew I needed money. She contacted me, offered a lot of money. I just needed to do a few things for her first."

"Like kill people?"

"I arranged the car bomb for Hannah, the hexed donor for Benoit, even organized the cruises, but she dropped off the tickets. I got a great deal on that singles' cruise. Your aunts will love it."

He seemed almost eager to please. Wanted Xandie's thanks for a job well done. Elspeth really could pick them. "And killing Henry, Minerva, and Bridget? Did they love what happened to them?"

"She hates Elspeth for what happened to her

father. Would have done anything for him. Even hiding from everyone who she truly was. Then her dad and her half-brother killed themselves. She stayed quiet and plotted. She's been planning this for a really long time. Once she has Elspeth's amulet piece, she'll destroy Paladin, PIG, and the supernatural world."

A sparkly blue and yellow cloud exploded with a pop over Whitburn. He screamed and grasped his throat, trying to speak. Pure babble streamed from his mouth. A look of horror spread over his face, and he fell to his knees.

Xandie rushed forward and grabbed him as he tried to force words out. "Purple nose donkey peak." He pounded on the ground. "Snark. Snarky bark." He pointed behind Xandie.

"He was always a talker. I could never shut him up. Now he can babble to the last breath in his body. And it *will* be the last. Your grandmother's babble hexes are elegant in their killing efficiency." Delilah from the diner, with her curves, platinum blonde beehive, and blood-red nails, stepped out onto the bluff, dragging a gagged and bound Elspeth Harrow.

Whitburn moaned aloud and toppled aside, dragging Xandie down to the ground.

"Can't say it's nice to see you, Delilah." Xandie

gently shook off Whitburn's hand and stood. She wasn't kneeling for anyone. Certainly not a fake blonde, blood-crazed killer.

"What? No exclamation of surprise? No *how could you?*" Delilah smiled.

"You're new to town, someone died in the diner you waitress in, and then you mysteriously disappear? And every time you saw me, you tried to pump me for information. It wasn't hard to make the connection. How did you trap Elspeth?"

Delilah dumped the rope she'd been leading Elspeth with onto the ground. "Typical. Always thinks she's smarter than everyone in the room. She never expected little old me to come wringing my hands about this poor wounded vampire I'd found. She didn't expect me to hit her on the back of the head with a rock." Delilah giggled, proud of her handiwork entrapping the unsuspecting Elspeth.

Xandie frowned at her grandmother who grunted behind the gag. "Frankly, that's disappointing on all counts, Elspeth. But as a gesture of goodwill, why don't you untie my grandmother and take me instead? I'm the Librarian."

"But she killed my father," Delilah sneered and kicked the old woman in the side. "She has what I want. What I need. I'll finish what my father started. And I don't care who I hurt to do it."

Elspeth dislodged her gag. "Killer Barbie got the jump on me, I'm ashamed to admit it." Elspeth shrugged. "Buchanan might have a point about my old bones. It would've never happened when I was young."

Hellacious drummed his feet against the ground and pointed at Delilah, babbling furiously.

"That's enough from you, Hell. Dead men tell no tales." Delilah threw a silvery round ball at the man, who stiffened and let out an undulating scream.

What the heck? Xandie scooted farther away from the hexed necromancer.

"Fear hex on top of the babbling hex. Plays torn from my very own hex book. Guess a lack of originality is something else you inherited from Proctor. Along with the psychotic gene."

Delilah bent down and spat on Elspeth. "You were always so dismissive of Father. You laughed behind his back and complained when he asked you to do the littlest thing. Then you reported to Paladin and killed him."

"Didn't he kill himself?" Xandie was positive Elspeth had said he'd died by his own hand. And something else confused her. Delilah's words sounded personal. Not just a grudge from an abandoned daughter or inherited hatred from a dead parent. But a personal hatred of someone who'd worked with Elspeth. Knew how her grandmother operated. Her distinctive hexes.

"Elspeth drove him to it. It's her fault my brother and father died."

"My husband died too. You're not the only one who lost family."

"You lost nothing," Delilah screeched at Elspeth but then managed to calm herself down. "That's going to change." Delilah sidled up to Xandie and patted her on the cheek. "You were so gullible, so nice to poor ol' Delilah. You had no idea who I was. And now you're going to help me get Elspeth's amulet piece." She smiled triumphantly.

"I don't think so, because I know your real name."

Delilah reared back, shock on her face at Xandie's words.

"That's right. I've worked out who you are. You're Alberta Burne, at least on your adoption records. I guess you decided since Whitburn used the alias Burne during World War Two, it was also a good way to implicate him further in any crime you committed. Throw us off the scent. You were also

Proctor's admin assistant and his daughter. You were adopted, but I guess you decided to use Hannah Lynch as an alias, just in case anyone found out Proctor had another child. I'm betting he didn't want anybody to find out who you were. You were the perfect mole. The coven's administrative assistant and Albert Proctor's illegitimate daughter." Xandie wished she'd seen this earlier.

"What?" Elspeth pushed herself to her knees. "A car bomb killed Hannah. Plus, she was a blue-eyed brunette beanpole. And she was a null—any hexes coming from her are nullified, canceled. She can't throw magic; she can't do magic. It's not possible."

Delilah, a.k.a. Hannah, walked behind Xandie and grabbed her hair, holding her in place. "Well, well, well. The Librarian is a bit of a smarty-pants. You're right, I *am* Hannah. Plastic surgery, a good hairstylist, a new eating plan, and a gullible witch willing to sacrifice her life force to neutralize my null barrier. I still can't do a lot of magic, but I can direct someone to brew a hex, so I can then throw it at my unsuspecting victims. I just went the extra mile like my father."

"Your father was a thief and a liar, and it doesn't look like the apple fell far from the tree," Elspeth sneered, wriggling like a worm on the hook to get at the ropes securing her wrists.

Delilah/Hannah put her head on Xandie's shoulder. "I get it. You hate to lose, Elspeth. But if you don't help me and give me the amulet piece, I'll flail every piece of skin off your granddaughter." Hannah towed Xandie along with her as she walked closer to Elspeth. They passed close to Whitburn, who still writhed on the ground, terrified. And babbling.

Xandie looked down as one particular word sounded almost like her name. Whitburn still shrieked, but a shred of sanity lingered in his eyes. He reached out a hand as Hannah frog-marched her past. Xandie forced her head straight and winked at Elspeth.

Whitburn latched onto Hannah's ankle and yanked hard.

Hannah screamed and stumbled back, letting go of Xandie who raced to the side of her grandmother.

Colin jumped out of the shadows and latched onto Hannah's skinny ankle with sharp teeth. He mumbled around the limb, "You won't hurt my Elspeth. Bah, you taste like tuna."

Screeching, Hannah danced around, shaking her leg like a crazed aerobics instructor.

Colin flew through the air and landed at the base of a large bush covered in shadows.

Xandie watched as a slim hand pulled the silent pug into the shadows. Maybe someone was watching out for them?

"You better not have hurt a hair on my prize-winning little boy. Or you'll regret it," Elspeth growled, her face lengthened slightly as her teeth grew canine points.

"Your cheap theatrics don't impress me. And I'm not surprised that monstrosity of an animal went down so easily. Isn't the old saying 'you get what you pay for?' Cheap and shoddy should be your middle name, Elspeth." Hannah sneered at the Harrow witch and rubbed her rapidly swelling ankle.

"At least I'm not a thief or a con artist *or a killer*. Both you and your father can lay claim to those titles."

"Filthy lies," Hannah screamed at Elspeth. "My father was an amazing man, and you killed him. Now all of you will pay." Hannah raised her hand and showed Elspeth a black ball. "Remember these, Elspeth? Absorber hex. The same hex my brother used to level Paladin Headquarters. These babies are the pride of my arsenal. Once I hit you with this, you'll absorb all the energy and electrical impulses around you until you go supernova. Poetic, I thought." Hannah raised a hand but screamed as a bullet came flying out of nowhere and hit her flesh.

"I think my mom might have something to say about you killing us."

A slim woman, with chin length brown hair and bright, amber eyes stepped out from the underbrush, rifle extended, Hannah in her sights.

Xandie knelt next to her grandmother and untied the last of Elspeth's knots. She stared at the shooter. *Miranda Harrow, my mother.* The woman seemed larger, more dangerous, but then, the last time Xandie had seen her mother was over twenty years ago, when she'd been five. Well, except for when the mysterious shooter had showed up in Harrow House's garden, and even then, she hadn't been certain it was her mother.

Elspeth scooted away from Xandie until she stood by herself. She held her empty hand up in the air. "Here I am, Hannah. The woman you hated most in this world. What ya gonna do about it?"

"I'll kill you. I don't care how long it takes. You and your family always ruin everything. My plan, my life, *my* family."

Miranda noted where Elspeth now stood and hefted the gun to her shoulder.

A raised scar on the side of her mother's face from her temple down past her jawline mesmerized Xandie. Whatever had happened to her mother, she hadn't escaped unharmed. Heck, Xandie had no clue if her mother even remembered her.

"What do we have here? Seems like I'm not the only one feeling unkind to the Harrow bloodline." Head ASP agent sauntered out onto the bluff, a trio of younger agents behind him.

"Let me guess, the humans want a piece of me, too? Or is it my amulet you're after?" Hannah sneered and waved at the three pieces of the amulet strung around her neck. "You're out of luck. These are useless for widespread use until that hag gives up the last piece."

The black-suited agent strolled up to Xandie. He smirked and tapped her forehead with two fingers. "Nope, if you have a beef with the Harrows, have at it. I just want these two." He pointed to Xandie and her mother. "I couldn't care less what happens to anyone else or whatever shonky supernatural artifact you're after."

He leaned in, and Xandie smelled the stale onions he'd eaten as he whispered to her, "Told you. I'm like a bad penny. I always turn up and get what I want. You lose, Harrow."

Miranda smiled, her teeth uncannily similar to Elspeth's now sharply pointed canines. "Oh, I wouldn't say that, Malcolm. You know I'm always prepared, and this time I brought friends." She gestured with a jerk of her jaw. With a swirl of wind, a group of gold dragons materialized in human form next to the younger ASP agents. "Remember these gentlemen? Turns out they have a prior acquaintance with you. They were delighted to answer my call for reinforcements."

A young, muscled man with a shining crop of bright gold hair bowed to Xandie. "Ladon sends his compliments. He couldn't be here, but he sent his best guards to help with a little ASP clean up."

Ladon was a Hesper, a gold dragon who'd helped Xandie when dragon matriarch, Marjorie Penne, was poisoned. He'd escorted the same ASP agents away when they had tried to force her to act as bait for her mother.

"You see, Malcom, I did some digging while I recuperated at Paladin Inc. All your funding's been pulled. An investigation has dug up very illegal ASP practices. Your cronies are in jail, and there's a warrant out for you and your thugs. You're finished and so is your hold on me and mine."

Malcolm spat on the ground and raised a black 9-

millimeter Sig Sauer pistol and pointed it at Miranda. "I will take you down before I let you take me in."

"Oh, I have nothing to do with it." She pointed over his head.

A loud screech overhead had Malcolm flinching, his weapon forgotten, as golden claws plucked him off the ground. The dragon soared into the night sky, a thunder of dragons behind the leader, all carrying a cursing ASP agent each.

"The dragons have orders to drop the ASP asses to Paladin Headquarters. They won't be seeing the sun for a long time." Miranda grinned and hefted her rifle to her shoulder again.

"Neither will you." Hannah raised her hand, her little black ball clasped tight. "I'm sick of all these interruptions. This is about me and my father's revenge against the Harrow bloodline. You're all going to die, and I can't wait to enjoy the sight." The Morrigan killer calmly raised her hand above her head, letting the Harrows take in the sight of the onyx-colored ball.

"Geronimo."

"Oh no." Still kneeling where a bound Elspeth had lain, Xandie covered her eyes as Theo the cat, with his pet imp, Horatio, pounded to a halt in front of Hannah. The imp brandished a sharp shiny toothpick sword.

"Interfering humans, a talking cat, and a dead woman with a gun? This is all you've got?" Hannah screeched her defiance and drew her arm back to throw the hex. Just in time, a shaggy brown bear bounded over the top of her, knocking the killer to the ground.

The shaggy brown bear lumbered across to Xandie and shoved her gently down with a massive shoulder. He plonked next to her and shielded her with his bulk.

He must have stood at least eight feet tall on his hind legs, but laid out next to her, he looked like a shaggy mound of muscle. The bear had a distinctive shoulder hump and a large dish-shaped face. And the animal was currently making a purring noise as it tried to nuzzle into her.

"Braun?" The bear made a huffing noise Xandie took for assent. "Wow, you really don't need to worry about winter clothing, do you?" She ran a hand over his warm, shaggy coat.

Hannah slapped the ground. "No, I refuse to let you win, Harrow."

"For goodness sakes, woman. Put a hex in it." Buchanan flicked off an invisible barrier hex, as

Jackson and their agents blocked Hannah's access to Xandie and her family. A semicircle of muscled men enclosed Hannah, forcing the hex bombs from her hands. Buchanan handcuffed her with spelled manacles. "We all missed this one. The intelligence branches will get an ass whooping."

He handed Hannah Proctor off to one of his men, no squabble over jurisdiction necessary as Braun was in bear form. Buchanan stood in front of Elspeth and gently lifted her to her feet. "I swear you're harder to hag-sit than Houdini."

"I have skills, and I'm not afraid to use them. I could have taken her, but Xandie would have ended up as collateral damage. I'm not losing any more family members." Elspeth's gaze shot to a stiff Miranda Harrow, who looked as though she'd disappear again at any moment.

Buchanan followed her gaze. "Go easy on her. She still doesn't have all her memories back yet. I found out that Paladin Inc. had been hiding her until she was one hundred percent recovered, but like you, she refused to stay hidden."

Elspeth harrumphed. "Harrows have minds of their own."

Buchanan snorted. "Really? I would never have guessed that."

Miranda Harrow stepped closer to Xandie and cocked her head. She handed her rifle off to a leather-clad agent and moved forward until she stood in front of Xandie and her tame bear shifter. She crouched and reached a trembling hand out to her daughter's cheek.

Xandie held her breath, her nerve endings twitching. "Mommy?" Her world teetered on the edge of a sob.

Miranda Harrow ran a hand over Xandie's disheveled hair. "I couldn't remember you for such a long time. But there was a gaping hole inside me. Something or someone was missing. Then I heard about this new Librarian in Point Muse, finding bodies and solving mysteries. It shocked a few memories loose. Little things were coming back. By then, I'd already run from ASP and Paladin Inc. took me in. I don't remember everything, but I know I love you, Xandie." She looked at Elspeth. "You, too, Mom."

Elspeth sniffed as a tear ran down her wrinkled cheek. "Has anyone seen my hipflask?"

Xandie let relief flow through her and bellowed out a snort of laughter, joined eventually by her mother and Elspeth.

The PIG and Paladin agents started squabbling

over who'd walk Hannah Lynch down to the waiting SUVs but ceased sniping at each other for a moment to stare at the Harrow women cackling like a trio of ancient witches. It was enough to make them all take giant steps backward.

With a popping of joints, the bear's form shivered and shrank down to a human-sized, naked police chief.

Xandie blinked a few times but hastily averted her eyes when her newly found mother cleared her throat and moved both of them out of touching distance. She'd always known Zach Braun was a large-shouldered man. Now she knew there was not an ounce of fat on him, only pure muscle. Xandie fanned her now flaming cheeks. Suddenly, the prospect of a coffee date with the police chief was a little more serious.

Jackson strode over to the shifter and threw his ankle length overcoat at the naked man. "For Hecate's sake and all of our future mental states, cover up." The PIG agent switched his gaze to Xandie and then sighed when he caught her watching them. "A guy knows when he's beat. Happy hunting, shifter."

The agent strolled up to Xandie and her mother. He inclined his head in greeting to the silent

Miranda Harrow. "The Paranormal Investigative Group has ceded all control of the situation and any information pertaining to the Morrigan Coven over to Paladin Inc. Our involvement ends here."

"No reason to stay in Point Muse then?" The man had infuriated her with his wiping of her memory and the fact that PIG had a file on her. But without him, she'd never have found the Harrows and her mother or Theo.

"No. Everything's resolved. *Everything.*" He stared at Braun for a moment before turning back. "But if you ever need me, I mean PIG, just call." He doffed an imaginary hat to the Harrows in a salute and ambled off.

"Jackson?" Xandie called out, causing him to turn back. "Thank you. For all your help."

He waved and disappeared with some of the Paladin agents and the handcuffed Hannah Lynch.

Braun slipped the overcoat on and stretched, making sure it covered his naked body. He winked at Xandie when he caught her watching.

Xandie fought the fiery blush spreading over her cheeks and nodded her thanks for his furry protection. *The bear shifter is growing on me.*

She switched her attention back to her family. Miranda had made her way over to Elspeth, and they stood holding hands, quietly conversing. It was surprising when the two women stood next to each other how strong the family resemblance was. The same Harrow eyes, the same stubborn chin, and that glint in the eye of mischief and mayhem. Her mother's had dimmed, but hopefully it wouldn't take long for her to regain all her memories. Elspeth would see to that. How they'd explain this to Xandie's staid, normal father, she had no idea. But that was a problem for the future.

"It's okay. I'm all good. Now let me at that killer dame." Colin wobbled out from under the bush, swaggering like he was drunk on Witchshine until he found Buchanan's feet. Where he collapsed with a loud, reverberating belch. Followed by an outpouring of tuna-scented muck on the Paladin's boots. "That quack, Amelia, might be right. I don't think fish agrees with me."

"Elspeth!" Buchanan bellowed and cursed as he shook the tainted mess off his feet.

Her grandmother just cackled and completely ignored the Paladin. A normal state of affairs for the duo.

Xandie nodded, exhausted but relieved. The world was back to normal...as normal as Point Muse could get.

Elspeth was safe, her mother returned, and a killer uncovered.

Another Point Muse murder solved...

For now.

The end.

***

Want More?

You can sign up for my mailing list. It's for new releases and no spam. Be the first to grab specials, new releases and freebies.

Sign up now.

https://www.kellyethan.com/newsletter

NEWSLETTER

Want more?

You can sign up for my mailing list. It's for new releases and no spam. Be the first to grab specials, new releases, and freebies.

Sign up now.
https://www.kellyethan.com/newsletter

LEAVE A REVIEW

Did you like this book?
Please leave a review for it on Amazon!

The Cursed Crow and the Deadly Hex

ABOUT THE AUTHOR

I want to thank everyone who spent the time to read my novel.

My world is small town magic, mystery and mayhem, with plenty of snarky laughs along the way.

With an overactive imagination and a love of all things that go bump in the night, it was natural to write cozy paranormal mysteries, but I also love paranormal romance. No matter the genre, I love sarcastic heroines who like to save the day and solve the puzzle.

With a busy and chaotic household, writing is my outlet for madness. I live in Australia and when not writing, I can be found plotting my next fictional murder or chasing after the family's ferocious hellhound.

Visit me today at my website or say hello on social
media.

Website:

https://www.kellyethan.com

facebook.com/KellyEthanWriter

instagram.com/kellyethanauthor

tiktok.com/@authorkellyethan

ALSO BY KELLY ETHAN

COZY PARANORMAL MYSTERY:

Point Muse Cozy Paranormal Mystery Series

The Wicked Witch and the Christmas Chaos

The Wicked Witch and the Stolen Snow Globe

The Conniving Carver and the Jeering Jack-O-Lantern

The Wicked Witch and the Ultimate Smackdown

The Wicked Witch and the Abominable Snowman

The Wicked Witch and the Killer Grinch

#0 The Pernicious Pixie and the Choked Word

#1 The Killer Knight and the Murderous Chairleg

#2 The Dastardly Dragon Killer and the Poison Breath

#3 The Murderous Monster and the Stony Gaze

#4 The Cursed Crow and the Deadly Hex

#5 The Slanderous Siren and the Grievous Gift

#6 The Vengeful Villain and the Cursed Treasure

#7 The Fiendish Foe and the Deadly Jewels

#8 The Nefarious Nemesis and the Wedding Jinx

Point Muse Cozy Paranormal Mystery Boxed Set: Books 1-3

Point Muse Cozy Paranormal Mystery Boxed Set: Books 4-6

Point Muse Cozy paranormal Mystery Boxed Set: Books 1-8

LILA HARROW: Point Muse Cozy Paranormal Mystery

Cookies, Curses and Christmas Corpses.

#1 Cupcakes, Corpses and Chaos

#2 Pies, Potions and Peril

#3 Sin, Sugar and Shadows

LILA HARROW Point Muse Boxed Set: Books 1-3

HOLLY HARROW: Point Muse Cozy Paranormal Mystery

Banshee, Vikings and Voodoo

#1 Banshee, Death and Disarray

#2 Banshee, Moonshine and Madness

#3 Banshee, Sea Monster and Sabotage

HOLLY HARROW Point Muse Boxed Set: Books 1-3

Non Fiction

Heart and Craft.